GW00771893

Anne of
Athelhampton
and the
Queen's Pearls

2

*The second book in the
Anne of Athelhampton
trilogy*

Anne of Athelhampton

and the

Queen's Pearls

Giles Keating

Illustrated by

Noah Warnes

First Published in Great Britain by
Athelhampton Press
Athelhampton
Dorchester
Dorset
DT2 7LG
United Kingdom

1st edition

Copyright © 2023 Giles Keating

A catalogue entry of this book is available from the
British Library

ISBN 978-0-9555815-5-7

*All rights reserved. No part of this book may be reproduced or transmitted in
any form or by any means, electronic or mechanical including photography,
recording or any information storage and retrieval system, without permission
in writing from the publisher*

Illustrations by Noah Warnes

Designed by Owen Davies

Printed the United Kingdom by Henry Ling Limited,
at the Dorset Press, Dorchester, DT1 1HD

Available in the usual stockists
or order online
www.athelhampton.co.uk

Table of Contents

Characters		ix
Map of The Martyns' Dorsetshire, 1580s		x
Chapter 1	Harvest Supper	1
Chapter 2	On the Clifftop with Bayard	9
Chapter 3	Chidiock's Poem	23
Chapter 4	William Arundell's Proposal	29
Chapter 5	The Ghost	37
Chapter 6	Dorchester Market	47
Chapter 7	Plot and Counter-Plot	61
Chapter 8	Young John	71
Chapter 9	The Privy at Almer	83
Chapter 10	Cumberground	93
Chapter 11	Unexpected News at the Party	101
Chapter 12	Old Wardour Castle	111
Chapter 13	A Most Notable Coward	125
Chapter 14	The Second Parchment	137
Chapter 15	The Letter from Captain Heynes	149
Chapter 16	Red Sky at Night	159
Chapter 17	The Upright Man	163
Chapter 18	The Executioner	181
Chapter 19	But a Frost of Cares	195
Chapter 20	St Giles-in-the-Fields	199
Chapter 21	The Scaffold	203
Chapter 22	Westminster Abbey	213
Epilogue		223
Historical Notes *(warning: contains spoilers)*		229
Acknowledgements		233
Biographies		235

Principal Characters

Anne Martyn, *of Athelhampton, Dorsetshire*
Jane, *Anne's sister*
Chidiock Tichborne, *Jane's husband*
Eliza, *Anne's sister*
Henry Brune, *Eliza's husband*
Sir Nicholas and Lady Margaret, *Anne's parents*
Sir George Bingham, *Anne's uncle*
'Young John' Tregonwell, *Anne's cousin*
Lizzie Moryshe, *Anne's friend*
Robert Devoll, *Lizzie's sweetheart*
William Arundell
Captain Stephen Heynes
Walter Bearde

Other Characters

Frances, *Anne's sister*
'Little Elizabeth', Janie and Marie, *Eliza's children*
Nathan, *a servant at Tyneham Manor*
The late Lady Elizabeth, *Anne's paternal grandma*
The late 'Old Sir John' Tregonwell, *the Lady
    Elizabeth's second husband*
Joan Wadham, *Anne's maternal grandma*
Master David Bond, *steward of Athelhampton*
Humphrie Devoll, *Robert's brother*
Ma Melemouth
Master Moryshe, *Lizzie's father*
Roger Munday, *Captain Heynes' bosun*
Mistress Munday, *Roger's wife*
Anthony Floyer
Master Blanke, *jeweller*
The Baron Dacre

The Martyns' Dorsetshire 1580s

Lydlich

Athelhampton

Dorchester

River From

Durdle Door

N
W
E
S

Fyddleford ↗ Wardour

Mylton Abbey
• Mylton

• Almer

River Piddle

uddle

ool • Bindon
Abbey

• Wareham

Purbeck

Corfe
Castle
•

• Tyneham

Swanage →

Worbarrow
Bay

Brandy
Bay

ANNE OF ATHELHAMPTON

Chapter 1

Harvest Supper

One stockinged foot perched precariously on the top rung of the ladder, Anne turned to pin the corn dolly to the wall and almost lost her grip as she caught the glare of her brother-in-law Chidiock. He was staring at her from the far end of the Great Hall, the twin ginger sheaves of his beard unmistakable among the farmers heaving baskets of fruit. In his hand he held a parchment and she began to feel queasy as it reminded her of what had happened at Yuletide.

She slid to the ground, jumping past Lizzie's steadying foot on the bottom rung and saying, "Why do you think Chidiock's gawping at me, after pretending for months and months that I didn't exist?"

"Do you think he's finally decided to try and have you punished for breaking the rules of the old religion?" said Lizzie, taking her foot off the ladder and straightening her servant's smock.

Peering between the yeomen milling around the Great Hall, Anne saw that Chidiock had turned away and was disappearing through a small door into the cellar, accompanied by the second of her brothers-in-law, Henry.

"If they are going to get me punished, I want to

know about it, so I can try and stop them. Let's listen to what they say!"

She gathered her fine woollen skirts above her ankles, ducked under garlands of poppies and clover and slipped through the archway in the corner of the Hall that led to the side stairs. At the top, she found the catch hidden in the wall panels behind the great four-poster bed, opened the concealed door and slipped into the mouse odoured space beyond. Behind, she heard Lizzie breathing hard, and felt something furry brushing past as she squatted to look through the cracks in the floorboards.

She could see Chidiock's red hair just beneath, barely a hand's span away, for the secret room she was in had been built directly above the low-ceilinged cellar. She heard him say, "...the flames will rally men to fight for the old religion, 'tis writ by..."

'Flames?' Lizzie mouthed the word soundlessly, frowning, and Anne shrugged her shoulders as the speaker lowered his voice and spoke an unfamiliar word, sounding like 'balifrey.'

Henry replied, "Three or four ships may lie in the bay, 'tis but a hundred paces to Tyneham Manor…" There came loud singing from the Great Hall, "*Hey derry derry, with a poupe and a lerry,*" and only when the noise subsided could he be heard again: "...'tis too important to trust to Anne, she is still young!"

Even as Anne squeezed her hands into fists, to stop herself shouting out at this, Chidiock lifted two scrolls that he carried, waving them excitedly and saying, "She's not too young. She's nearly at her thirteenth anniversary and if she grows a few more inches she will be as tall as thee!"

The two men vanished and Anne whispered, "It doesn't sound as though they want to punish me – it seems they want me to do something to help them."

"They talked about ships. But surely they don't want you to help them become smugglers, in place of the dead pirate captains, God rest their souls?"

"That seems unlikely! But I'll ask them!"

"Don't let them know we were eavesdropping. And best put thy shoes back on, they're just about to start the dancing!"

Anne stood up, stepped carefully past the black shape waiting patiently by a large mouse-hole and scurried back downstairs with Lizzie to the Great Hall, where the farmers were standing and cheering. A large red-faced yeoman climbed on a table, struck a copper gong with a mallet and as the clang echoed from the rafters high above and other voices fell silent, he cried out: *"Time to dance, time to drink!/ And see ye do not spill/For if ye do/Ye shall drink two."*

Anne raced to grab the arm of Henry, who was filling his goblet with ale from a great barrel perched between baskets of apples and pears.

As the musicians on the gallery started up the Brawle, she led him into the melee of dancers and asked, "How fares it with thy kinsfolk at Tyneham Manor? Lizzie asked me, but I've never met them, 'tis too far for me to ride on my Jinty."

"They are well enough in themselves," said Henry, "but their livestock face a bad winter, for they cannot grow corn on their sea-swept farm. I fear they will pay high prices when they buy winter fodder."

"And might they earn a few shillings for corn by helping the smugglers?"

Henry looked at her, mouth open with astonishment. "My folk there adhere to the old religion, like me. 'Twould be an ungodly act to engage with smugglers and they would never do it, any more than I!"

The first round finished and Anne went across the floor to dance with Chidiock. But as she approached he grabbed the hand of a nearby farmer's wife instead. Anne put her hands on her hips and screwed up her face at him, and scurried over to Lizzie. "How can I talk with Chidiock? He's trying to avoid me!"

"I have a plan! You should dance with Robert!"

"With Robert? But how will that help? And won't you be jealous?"

"Of course not!" Anne felt her friend's eyes on hers and her hands being squeezed tight as the maidservant lowered her voice to a whisper. "We are to be betrothed, once he completes his apprenticeship. You are the first to know, don't tell anyone else yet!"

Smiling, Anne pulled Lizzie into a tight embrace, and kissed her on both cheeks. "I'm so happy for you both," she said, trying to keep her voice low.

The music started for the next dance and Anne whirled round the floor with Robert, enjoying the confident steps and bright blue eyes of her friend's sweetheart. They kept a few paces away from Lizzie, who was now dancing with Chidiock, but when the music paused they came up alongside. The maidservant put her partner's hand into Anne's, who held on tight, so that her red-bearded brother-in-law had no choice but to dance with her.

Anne swallowed hard and said, "I see fine parchments in the pouch at thy waist, are ye investing in a sea-voyage?"

Chidiock's brow creased and he said, "I'm not interested in ships, where did ye get that idea? Ye is the most inquisitive of my sisters-in-law, and sometimes that is a virtue, but not on this occasion!"

"But then, what are those parchments for?"

"Ye will find out in good time. One is for ye, but 'tis not yet ready. And now, I should not be dancing with ye! After thy bad behaviour at the Arundell's house!"

She glared at him. "I wasn't bad! You're cross because I didn't go to the Mass for the old religion. But just because you go, doesn't mean that I have to."

Anne sensed the chilliness in Chidiock's face as he broke off the dance in mid-song and strode away to a corner of the Great Hall, where he took the hand of his wife Jane, her second-eldest sister, whose beautiful emerald-green eyes were staring at her. She looked away, unable to bear the coldness, and let out a breath in relief as she felt her hand gripped by the warmness of Lizzie's. "Jane's become so much more distant to me since she married Chidiock, it's miserable, I was really happy for her when she got betrothed."

She felt her hand squeezed tightly by Lizzie, who said, "She's still your sister, you could try and find a quiet moment with her alone and ask her what's wrong. Now, let's find new partners and see who can keep dancing the longest!"

Anne nodded, but as she turned to find someone for the next round, her gaze alighted on Chidiock, who was now talking with Henry, and she saw the two of them looking at her, then at the parchments and then back at her, and she started to feel sick again.

Anne's legs were aching as the musicians struck up the Dumpe, the fast dance that marked the end of the evening, but she saw Lizzie take the hand of a bleary-eyed shepherd and anxious not to be left behind, she grabbed the arm of her black-bearded soldier uncle Sir George. She spun out across the half-empty dance floor with him, dodging the outstretched legs of a yeoman asleep by an upturned beer keg, and a pair of drunken farmers tottering across their path.

The musicians played their final notes and as they started to pack away their flutes and viols, Anne curtseyed to her uncle and flopped onto a chair next to Lizzie, saying, "We both held out to the end!"

"We outlasted Jane and Chidiock, Henry – almost everyone..."

"...And even thy Robert! Where is he?"

"He helped his fellows drain a barrel and fell asleep, over there! Come, let's make him comfortable."

Anne helped Lizzie put some straw under the sleeping mason's head, watched silently by Gyb, the black cat who had been mousing in the secret room. Sir George came over with some sacks, saying, "Here, use these to cover the lad's chest."

On impulse, Anne said to him, "Might I ask you a difficult question?" He stared at her hard without replying and she took a deep breath, squeezed Lizzie's hand, and said, "Pray tell me, what is 'balifrey'?"

The soldier's eyes seemed to darken and become almost invisible. "That is not a name to utter lightly," he said, and paused. For a moment Anne thought he would ask her where she had heard it, and then she understood that he would not ask, for he knew that she would lie and did not want to make her do that.

"That is 'Le Balafré'," Sir George continued, "in English it means Scarface, and 'tis the name given the Duke of Guise, mortal enemy of our good Queen Elizabeth. He has sworn to destroy her, and put Mary on the throne instead. Any man in England who deals with him would commit treason." His voice lightened and he added, "And now, 'tis time for God-fearing men to be abed, and I wish ye both good night."

Left alone with Lizzie, Anne found herself shivering as she said, "Chidiock and Henry are putting themselves in deepest danger, if what they're doing is connected with this 'Balafré.'"

"'Tis not smuggling, not voyaging. So, what can it be?"

"I don't know, but we're going to work it out. And find a way to stop them."

Chapter 2

On the Clifftop with Bayard

As Anne came into the stables, she caught the horse's dark eyes in hers: fifteen hands of fine stallion, his flanks the reddish brown of autumn leaves, the star-shaped birthmark on his left shoulder glowing in the morning sun. "Good morning, Bayard," she said softly as she stroked his head, and he replied with a gentle neigh. As a foal, he'd been set to develop into the perfect mount for her brother Christopher, after whose death some unknown quirk of nature had caused his growth to stop a hand short of what everyone had expected. Now, he was a man's horse scaled for a woman. He would be just the right mount for her, if only it was allowed.

Anne sighed and walked three stalls along to Jinty, the small gelding that she had ridden for more years than she could remember. She checked his oats and water and started to rub down his flanks as Humphrie, Robert's brother, came hurrying over, rubbing his eyes. "I'll do that for you, mistress Anne, I can rouse the others to help me."

"We'll do it together. Leave them to their slumbers."

A ray of early sun fell on the saddle as they lowered it onto Jinty, and Anne glanced outside to where a crimson glow silhouetted the stone apes on Athelhampton's roof.

"Red sky in the morning, shepherd's warning," said Humphrie, "'twill rain hard today."

A shadow blocked the stable doorway. Anne turned and saw it was her father, Sir Nicholas, with his hunting-dog Urian. She bent to stroke the hound and heard a deep voice echoing off the oak timbers of the stables, and looking up she realised that Sir George was there as well. He said, "Your father and I had some fine port wine last night, and we spoke of important things." Anne caught her breath; there was only one matter that might be announced in the stables, but she dared not hope for it. "After we talked of how Jinty is now well sized for thy little cousin, he went to speak with thy mother." She could barely breathe as he continued, "They have agreed that I shall be allowed to give thee Bayard."

"Sir George!" Anne curtseyed so low she felt her knees would touch the ground, as much to hide her excitement as to show the respect due to this announcement. "This is a most generous gift, which I accept with deepest thanks. And, dear Father, I thank you!"

"A fine rider needs a fine horse," said Sir Nicholas, "but 'tis not just that. I talked about it long and deep with thy mother last night, and we agreed that whatever we may permit or prohibit, you will somehow find trouble. And, when you do find trouble, 'tis best you have a good mount to get away from it, fast and clean."

Sir George laughed and said, "'Tis a wise father, that knows his own child! And now," he continued, looking at Anne, "some advice. With Bayard, tell him where ye wish to go, and who ye wants to see."

"Surely, he cannot understand what I say?" she said.

Sir George smiled and said, "Of course not. But he has travelled far and wide, and he remembers."

Anne rode her new mount out of the stables and turned right for the short journey to the Puddletown woods, where she could gather the acorns that her mother used for making dye. It was barely two miles, but would have taken thirty or forty minutes on poor Jinty, who would have been exhausted with her weight.

Bayard moved forward at a fast trot, and she saw that she would scarcely have time for breath before they arrived. The radius of her world had widened faster than her imagination.

Abandoning the idea of fetching acorns, she reined Bayard in and they came to a halt at Puddletown village green. Why not see whether Sir George was right about Bayard's memory? She leant forward, patted the horse's flank, and spoke into his ear.

"Let us go to Tyneham Manor."

Her mount bayed gently, set off on the lane out of the village and broke, unbidden, into a canter. She gripped the reins tightly and in moments they crested the brow of a hill, revealing a vista of the Frome river glinting far ahead as it flowed towards the distant Isle of Purbeck. She'd never been there but knew it was the stronghold of the pirates, the most powerful of whom had been Captain Stephen Heynes. It was where Endy, her pet ape, had first arrived in Dorsetshire, and at this reminder of him she sighed into the wind and had to squeeze her eyes to stop the dampness.

Half a mile further on, Bayard slowed at a crossroads and gently but firmly pulled against her grip to show that he wanted to turn right, away from the Purbeck road. Anne smiled – he really did seem to know the route she had asked for.

A fine modern house came into view, its white stonework as yet untouched by moss. 'This cannot be Tyneham,' thought Anne, 'for 'tis not by the sea.' But it was beside a fast-flowing river and her hands went clammy as she saw that the ancient bridge across to the far bank was blocked by a man standing in the middle, dressed in the white habit of a monk and standing with hands on hips, staring at her.

"Good morrow, my mistress." He spoke with a rasping tone that belied his fair words.

Anne swallowed hard, and replied, "Well met, good Friar. Pray tell me, this house is recently built by good craftsmen, who lives there?"

"'Twas where my master brought his bride when they were wed."

"'Tis a fine place for a honeymoon!"

"Aye, 'tis fitting for a man who has now inherited the title of Viscount Bindon. Now, stay awhile and watch me scourge the village yeomen." He opened the basket that he carried on his back and took out a bundle of birch rods, and began to slash with them at the empty air beside him as though practising a blow – but also making it even more difficult to pass.

Anne's breathing quickened, but he was barely taller than she was, and she was mounted. She said in a commanding tone, "Good Friar, beatings are not something that I want to watch. I wish ye good day," and she pulled on the reins and edged Bayard towards him. At first she thought he would not move, but Bayard seemed unafraid of the flailing birch and pushed forward gently yet firmly, and at last the monk yielded.

She rode on across the bridge as quickly as she could, and passed through a village of tumbledown cottages. Looking back she saw the white-clad figure gesturing at some farmers emerging from the houses, who were pulling logs behind them. She felt herself quivering as she wondered whether he might be blocking the route more decisively for her way home, but Tyneham Manor seemed the only place where the mystery of the ships could be solved, and she would not turn back now. She dug her boots gently into Bayard's flanks and he cantered up the steep slope that led away from the hamlet and towards the sea.

At the crest, there came salt in her nose and her mouth, which grew stronger as she rode on, up hills and down dells, before emerging on a high plain. Her breath shortened with excitement as she saw a manor house barely three hundred paces ahead, and realised it must be Tyneham. On the horizon beyond, there was a strip of dark blue water, separating the brightness of the sky from the greens of the fields and the whites of the sheep.

She rode up to the dwelling, looking at the strange arms of three birds and a horse above the door as she pulled the bell-rope. Around a side wall came a young shepherd, his white smock stained from his flock, his crook almost as high as Bayard's head. Beside him was a larger, older man in a leather jerkin, and Anne felt sick as she saw that he had a great brown, bloody scab in the middle of his bald head. Clearly, neither of these men was dressed in the fine clothes that Henry's kinsfolk would wear, and as she looked around there was no sign of anyone else.

The young man spoke, and Anne thought his voice had an almost musical tone. "Good morrow, fair mistress, what seek ye?"

"Good day, I am here for thy master."

"Then he is a lucky man, for 'tis not every day he has such a fair visitor."

"Can you take me to him?"

"Nay," said the shepherd, "for this very morning he is gone to Dorchester for three days, with his good wife and his father, to buy hay for the winter in the market."

"Since I cannot see thy master, might ye show me the different parts of the sea, for I have ridden a way and should be grateful to see what is to be seen?"

"Then 'twill be me who has the luck, to have thy company even for a short hour."

Anne dismounted, tethered Bayard to a post and left him drinking from a stone trough as the young man led her onto a narrow, stony track high above the sea. His taciturn older companion spoke for the first time, in a low, rasping voice: "I will check that post for ye, young mistress, it has been loose these times."

She watched him go over to Bayard but then had to turn and concentrate on the precipitous path, with the cliff soaring high on the landward side and plunging to the sea on the other. In places, there was barely space for a single man and there were rocks and stones to trip on. The shepherd spoke, raising his voice against the crash of the waves, "Take care, for the view is fine, but the cliffs fall straight down to the water, twenty rods or more, and look to your balance, the wind is westerly, which blows strong." Even as he spoke, there came a gust, and the darkness on the horizon seemed to move rapidly towards them.

They picked their way carefully round the blind corners of the narrow path and at last emerged onto a broad grassy field atop a headland that jutted into the sea. There were fine views to the bays on either side and a good cart-track leading inland.

Anne, breathing easier in this safer place, braced herself against the wind, and asked: "And what names do men give to the places here?"

The older man had caught up with them and said, "To the east is Brandy Bay, and there is good reason for the name, and over there, westward, is Worbarrow Bay, which could just as well take the name Port Bay."

Although Anne knew that the smuggling had stopped when Captain Heynes had died in the ocean and the other pirates been hanged, she decided that these names gave her licence to speak as though it continued.

"So," she said, "these havens supply the good people of Dorsetshire with the drinks they need! And to my eye, Worbarrow is the larger, with space there for three or four ships, but only one in Brandy Bay?"

"Most I ever saw was one ship and that not often," said the shepherd, "for they preferred to slip in and out quick and easy, and one ship is more difficult to catch than two or three. But that was some years back."

Anne opened her mouth to ask another question, but closed it quickly as a stab of brute fear ran through her, for the older man was staring directly at her with suspicion in his face, his tone even harsher than before as he said, "Ye is not planning a smuggling party, young mistress? For that is the work of men."

Anne realised she had been foolish to question the strangers, and she sought to divert the discussion. "I thank ye, good masters, I have no idea of ships, but I have heard of many wonderful places here. I am told there is one where the cliff makes an archway over the water?"

The shepherd said: "Aye, the Durdle Door, 'tis a mile or more over there."

His companion spoke again: "'Tis a dangerous walk to Durdle in this weather, for the rain is about to break. And 'tis slippery and narrow on the way back to your horse, young mistress. Be careful of the questions ye asks, for unbidden guests are often welcomest when they are gone. Many have fallen down the cliffs here, and are never seen again."

Anne felt her throat contract, for here she was, in a strong wind with these two men, and that narrow path along the clifftop to negotiate before she could regain the sanctuary of Bayard. The young man said: "Nathan, do not scare the young mistress, look how frightened she is."

"Sometimes, people is a-frighted for good reasons. The comings and goings of ships here is the business of no-one, save those who live here. Man or maid, when strangers come asking what happens in these bays, 'tis best we help them down there to have a closer look."

With these words, he came to Anne and grabbed her shoulders, and she screamed high and loud into the wind, unable to hide her primaeval terror. He started to haul her towards the cliff-edge, her hands trying to tear him away from her and her heels trying to drag on the ground. The shepherd was shouting "Leave her, Nathan, let her free!" Anne screamed again and dug deeper into the soft earth and for a moment they stopped. But her assailant was twice her weight and with a curse he heaved her feet out of the ground and swung round behind her, pushing her ahead of him and growling: "Here we go, young mistress, ye can count the space for ships as ye fly down," as he brought her to the very brink, the waves crashing into the rocks far below.

Then the shepherd was grabbing and punching the older man and forcing him to release his grip on Anne. She leapt away and ran, faster than she could ever believe possible, desperate to find the way back to Bayard but terrified that she would pitch herself off the narrow path in her haste, for now the clouds had opened and the rain was making the rocks as slippery as ice.

Behind her, she heard the crack of bone on bone, and guessed that her young protector had been struck by the larger man, whose steps she heard approaching behind her. His shout came loud: "Ye have no hope, young mistress!"

She heard him curse as he slipped, but dared not look back for fear of a misstep, and after a moment his steps came again. She rounded a corner and saw Bayard by his post, but he was two hundred paces away and to reach him she had to follow the dangerous track in a great curve inland and out again. She screamed out loud, "Bayard," before the twist of the path took her out of his sight again.

A stone struck her arm and she winced with the pain as she realised that her pursuer was trying to make her lose balance. As another hit her leg, she found herself praying out loud, her voice clear against the wind: "*O, Lord God, heavenly Father, the Lord of Hosts, without whose providence nothing proceedeth, and without whose mercy nothing is saved; have mercy upon thine afflicted servant…*"

The brutal Nathan must have heard, for his voice came close behind her, crying out in a horrid tone, "Save thy prayer for the flight down the cliffs, young mistress,'twill serve thee better then."

But he was not the only living being to have heard her. A great brown shape appeared round a corner twenty paces ahead, sure-footed on the vertiginous path. Bayard approached, moving faster than she would ever dare on the slippery stones. His halter trailed loose, and she found herself wondering whether it had slipped accidentally or whether Nathan had deliberately undone it, falsely thinking that her mount would race away and leave her alone.

Either way, Bayard was here, and for a moment she slackened her pace and felt her limbs relax at the thought of escape. But a second later, her throat tightened as she realised that the track was too narrow for him to come alongside to let her mount. With him in front of her, Nathan would come up behind and seize her.

Bayard bore down on her without slowing and

suddenly she understood what she must do. She flattened herself against the cliff, pressing herself into nothing, as when she and Lizzie and Robert had hidden in impossibly small spaces behind the barrels in Master Bond's cellars at Athelhampton. Bayard eased beside her, hooves half out into the void, and stopped, his flank pressed hard against her, filling the complete width of the track.

Nathan came up to him, unable to get past and trying to grab him, but Bayard opened his mouth, bared his teeth and let out a deafening noise into the attacker's ear. Anne, spurred by fear, put one foot on a boulder and somehow began to wiggle herself up though the narrow gap between the cliff and the horse. Her riding-kirtle tore as it scraped against rock and she felt a searing pain as a stone cut through her stocking and into her shin.

At last her hand was across the saddle and with a great heave she pulled half her body flat onto his back. Now her foot was caught and she gave a scream of panic, but as she pulled she felt it come out of the boot, and finally she was fully on Bayard, clinging on for life. He pushed forward at her opponent, who was forced to retreat backwards along the precipitous path, lest he met the fate he had intended for her.

They came out onto the broader area of open land, where the shepherd lay inert, and Nathan, at last able to get to the side of the stallion, reached out to try to grab Anne and pull her down. Bayard caught him a terrible blow with his leg and then they were away. She hauled herself upright into a proper riding position in the saddle and pressed her legs harder than she ever thought she would into a horse's flanks. He sped through the sheeting rain as though he had wings, onto the safe, broad path that led inland.

Anne glanced back at the terrifying cliff-edge and the murderous assailant, gasping with relief at her escape, and starting to wonder about why he had attacked her. Was he always hostile to strangers who asked about ships? Or was he being especially protective about the secrets of the bay, because of what Chidiock and Henry were plotting?

ANNE OF ATHELHAMPTON

Chapter 3

Chidiock's Poem

"**P**oor thing! Thy clothes are more water than wool!" The Lady Margaret embraced her youngest daughter tightly, mindless of her soaking wet riding-kirtle and her blooded, mud-caked legs, one of them bootless. "Lizzie, where is the best fire?"

"In the Marriage Chamber, my Lady. Chidiock and Jane slept there last night, 'twas blazing when they left, scarce an hour ago."

"We'll go there. Be kind enough to bring us some warm water and dry clothes."

In the Marriage Chamber, Anne's mother drew up a stool for her by the fire and gently eased the torn and bloody hose off the foot that had lost its boot.

"Now, dear, tell me what happened."

Anne shivered, despite the warmth of the fire, at the thought that her mother might ban her from Bayard when she heard what had happened. But she didn't want to tell an outright untruth. "I went to look at the sea, and a horrid man attacked me. But Bayard saved me! I scraped my leg and lost my boot, but I got on his back and escaped."

She felt the Lady Margaret looking straight into her eyes, and then turning away and nodding slowly. She relaxed, as she recognised this sequence from the past: it was a way of saying: 'I know you haven't told me everything, but I trust you, and I know you have told me enough.' Out loud, her mother said, "You are home and safe, that's what matters. Now, let's get that wound cleaned."

Anne winced as the damp cloth was rubbed back and forth across the cut, but her mother nodded as she looked at it, saying: "'Tis not too deep, 'twill heal nicely. You'll barely notice it tomorrow when William Arundell comes."

Anne frowned. "William Arundell? I've only spoken with him a few times."

"I received a letter this morning. He's keen to see you. He would make a very suitable husband."

"But I'm too young to be married!" Anne felt her hands starting to shake. "And, after Young John turned out to be such a horrid suitor, Father promised that I could decide for myself!"

"Of course you can choose." The Lady Margaret's voice was calm. "But I think you'll like William, he seems a kind and pleasant man."

"He'll say I'm not wealthy enough, without Grandma's pearls!"

"He won't worry about that, he's got plenty of money of his own."

"Even if he does want me, I'm not ready for him!" She looked round the room, remembering the times she'd come to it for the first sight of her tiny nieces and nephews, who'd all been born here. "And, I'm not ready to have my own babies! I want plenty of time to ride on Bayard and be free, before I get married!"

"Even if you got betrothed soon, you wouldn't actually get married for quite a while. So, talk with

William and see how you feel. And now you should have some supper, you must be ravenous after all that riding."

The Lady Margaret turned and left the room and Anne, feeling her stomach rumbling, laced up a fresh kirtle as quickly as she could and managed to pull on her house shoes without disturbing her wound. She hurried downstairs to the Great Hall where her nieces were eating supper, supervised by Eliza, her eldest sister.

Little Elizabeth, who was the tallest of the children, reaching almost to Anne's shoulders, jumped up from the dinner table and her three much smaller siblings copied her. They all cried out in unison: "Aunt Anne, good evening, Aunt Anne!"

"But you must just call me Anne, for I'm not yet old enough to be Aunt!" she replied, and they all burst out laughing.

"Now, children, sit down and eat up your supper," said Eliza.

"Yes, mother," said the children together.

Anne squashed in on the bench next to Eliza, who said to her, "Chidiock asked me to give you this parchment – with his apologies for not handing it over himself. He and Jane left early."

"It's a pity that I missed them," said Anne.

"Jane…" Eliza hesitated before continuing, "…said that she wanted to leave while you were still out. She seems cross with you, I don't know what it's about."

Anne looked down at the table. "It's so sad having a fight with her! She's angry because I didn't go to Mass at Yuletide, she's hardly said a word to me since." She lifted her head and looked at Eliza. "I'll have to find a way to make it up to her, so we can be happy together, like I am with you and Frances."

Little Elizabeth had been examining the parchment carefully, and now she said, "Please, may we look at this? It must be important, for 'tis wrapped in rare ribbon and writ on vellum – Friar Wytterage never uses that in our lessons!"

"But why has Chidiock given such a special thing to me?" said Anne.

"He said 'tis because you are the most inquisitive among us four sisters," said Eliza, "and because you know William Arundell."

Anne shook her head. "But I don't! I only met him a couple of times, when we stayed with his family at Yuletide. Though he seems to be interested in me! And I wonder what the connection is between him and Chidiock?" She undid the ribbon, unwound the scroll, cleared her throat and read out loud:

"The time may come when sun shines not so
*   bright*
Go then where thee as babe and babes of thine
*   confine*
North-West the bells may ring no more
North-East the Symonds castle falls."

"What does it mean?" said Little Elizabeth.

"Maybe it doesn't mean anything," said Eliza. "Chidiock is a poet, and poets choose words for many reasons."

"I think it's a riddle"!" said Little Elizabeth,

jumping off the bench in excitement. "I've got one answer already: *where thee as babe and babes of thine confine* means Athelhampton, because I was born here, in the Marriage Chamber, and so were Janie and the little ones, and I'm sure you must have been as well, Aunt Anne!"

"Very good solving," said Eliza with a big smile.

"And perhaps the other lines refer to places at points of the compass," said Anne, joining in the excitement by bouncing up and down on the bench.

"You must show it to Lizzie, she's really good at solving riddles," said Little Elizabeth, who'd been looked after by Lizzie when she was small, and still treated her as a kind of big sister.

"I will," said Anne. "And listen, there's more." She turned the parchment over and continued reading aloud:

> "*South-East a Lord now wears the monkish robes*
> *South-West a family mansion looking out to sea*
> *And where waves wash an ancient door*
> *Therein ye find the key to set the blameless free*"

Anne stopped reading and fell silent, and she felt her hands go clammy as she thought to herself: 'The *family mansion looking out to sea* must be Tyneham, because none of our other relatives lives near the coast. But why does Chidiock want to get me involved in what's happening there?'

ANNE OF ATHELHAMPTON

Chapter 4

William Arundell's Proposal

William, an arm's length from her on the bench, said, "Mistress Anne, I thank you for gracing me with your time. 'Tis a pleasure to be in your company."

Anne was striving to keep her breathing steady. "My Lord William, I am most pleased to welcome you." Beyond him she saw her mother, watching as propriety required, but at a discreet fifty paces away on the other side of the lawn.

"To be honest," he leaned slightly towards her, "'tis a relief to me, to escape Wardour, which is old and cold."

Anne could not help laughing. "I feel just the same! I so much prefer Athelhampton, because it's modern and warm. Though your house is large and magnificent."

"My father loves it and has done many works to improve it, but I spend time away when I can. And I'm especially glad to be with you – and where could be better than this delightful setting by your wonderful dovecote?"

Anne looked up at the birds flying back and forth, and smiled. "I will ask Mother whether cook can prepare some for you today!"

"That is most kind of you, since I am partial to roast doves." He edged closer to her on the bench and said, "Now, I have an important matter to discuss. You have great qualities, which are scarce seen in one so young, indeed, are rare in anyone. You watch, you see, you listen, you understand."

Anne's breath tightened. Surely he was not about to propose marriage after such a short acquaintance? If he did, how could she explain that she was far too young, without being rude?

"At Wardour," William continued, "when the secret door into the chapel was opened so that everyone could go in and hear Mass for the old religion, you did not go in – you were always busy, advising the maids on care of your small nephews and nieces, or some such. So, it seems you are for the new religion, and against the old."

Anne's eyes widened at this sudden change of tone. She'd heard of people who'd been arrested for saying the wrong thing about religion, and was even less keen to talk about it than she was about marriage. "My Lord, might we perhaps talk of less serious matters, with the sun shining and the doves so pretty?"

William coughed. "I have not come here to talk about romance. I don't know why you might think that."

"At Wardour, you asked me to dance."

"And so did every man there, and that was no surprise, given thy beauty. But I have no interest in marriage with anyone – if I did, I would be most flattered if you would consider me."

"Yet, my mother said that you did have such an interest!"

"And there, I must confess some guilt," William averted his eyes, "for though I never said that to her, nor did I disabuse her when her thoughts turned that way."

"You hinted to her that you were a suitor, in order to get time alone with me! What do you want from me?"

"I am engaged in a mission, in which I wish to involve you."

"What kind of mission?" She felt a hollowness growing in her stomach.

"I try to help my good father retain the trust of our dear Queen. 'Tis not always easy, given that my grandfather was executed for foul treason."

"Surely you should persuade your father to stop holding Mass under the old religion – since that is prohibited!"

"Her Majesty is prepared to overlook this, as his one and only failing. But she is not so indulgent towards my uncle Charles, who is a fanatic in the old religion, like my late grandfather. And so, I make it my business to watch him."

Anne's breath was racing. She had promised herself to save her brothers-in-law from their own dangerous plans, but had no wish to be involved with these religious disagreements. "There's nothing I can do to help watch your family. So, no more need be said, and we can take a game of croquet, for the lawn is fresh cut and 'twill keep us warm!"

She made to stand up, but William looked at her and said, "Pray wait. My uncle, who lives abroad, goes much further than merely believing in the old religion – he wants to make everyone else go back to it! He is actively engaged to damage dear England and our most gracious Queen Elizabeth, because she supports the new religion. He plots to bring Mary to the throne instead, since she would restore the old religious ways."

Anne stared at William, her mouth open. "But that is treason!"

"'Tis most heinous treason, and still the tale gets worse, for he conspires with the Duke of Guise, who has sworn to destroy our dear Queen."

"Scarface!" Anne said this word and then wished she had not.

"Ah! You know of this villain. Who has told you this?"

"I do not recall."

"I hope you will remember soon. My traitorous uncle is plotting, with this evil Duke, to organise a raid with three or four ships on the coast here in Dorsetshire. They would kidnap some men and set fire to buildings. They do it to show strength and draw men to their cause – it is only the first step in their plot to put Mary in power."

Anne found William's eyes watching her closely. She tried to keep a steady gaze and give nothing away, though her heart was pounding, for now she understood the awful answer to the mystery of the last few days. Chidiock and Henry's conversation about Scarface and ships meant that they were involved in planning this treacherous seaborne raid.

She dug her fingers into her palms, furious with her brothers-in-law. Like William's uncle Charles, they not only believed in the old religion, but were trying to bring it back by doing terrible things. That

could put them, and maybe Jane and Eliza, in danger from the authorities.

William was continuing: "As a loyal servant of our Queen, I make sure that any of my uncle's talk and correspondence about such foul treasonous plots is communicated to her government."

Outraged, now, at what William was doing, Anne pushed her nails in even harder. "You mean that you spy on your own family!"

"That is a strong word, mistress Anne. All that I do is to pass on information."

"And you would wish me to pass on information about my family?" Anne saw her mother standing now, talking to Eliza.

"With the efforts you take to avoid Mass, you make very clear where your loyalties lie, and I am asking you to support those loyalties."

Anne breathed deeply and said, "I am loyal to our good Queen, and I am also loyal to my family." The Lady Margaret and Eliza were walking towards them now, and Anne began to pray silently that their steps would be faster.

"And what if one of your family was to engage in treason?" William was staring into her eyes as he asked.

Anne did not reply. She had been honest about her loyalties, she thought, for she had already resolved that she herself would stop Chidiock and Henry's plans. If she succeeded, she would save them – while also protecting her Queen.

Eliza was walking quickly, leaving the Lady Margaret behind. As she approached, William pressed his questioning even harder: "Or if you should hear words that might be construed as treason?"

Eliza arrived and interjected: "I have persuaded Mother to join us in a game of croquet, so we have four! Come, you have sat there talking for so long, let us take some sport!"

Anne jumped up and smiled. "What a good idea! And as for teams, let us two play together, for I am sure William is by far the best player, so let us put him with dear Mother. Then we have an even match!"

Anne seized her sister's hand and raced off with her to the edge of the lawn, resolving to spend not a moment more alone with William, who she saw staring at her with a frown as she lifted the mallets and balls from their wooden box.

Chapter 5

The Ghost

"William still hasn't gone!" Lizzie said quietly, as she crept into Anne's room. "He spent ages quizzing the servers while he was eating, then he put on his coat and went into the courtyard. I thought he'd go - but he's there now, talking with your father and some strange man who's just arrived. They keep gesturing at some packages piled up in a cart."

"He won't have learnt anything from the servers - we're the only ones who know what Chidiock and Henry are up to."

"Do you wish that you'd never agreed to meet him?"

Anne put down the sock that she'd been darning and looked directly at Lizzie, her face breaking into a smile. "Actually, I'm glad that I saw him again."

"But why? He tried to make you into a spy."

"I'm glad I saw him, because he's a very charming man. I think he's dangerous – and I don't want to marry him, nor him, me – but even so, I enjoy his company. Now, look what I've been doing while hiding up here!"

Anne went over to her chest, lifted out a pile of clean smocks and some neatly-folded kirtles and from under them produced a sheet of parchment, with a small tear in one corner.

"One of your old bits of schoolroom work?"

"Yes, but it only had a few bits of Latin on it. Most of it was blank, so there's plenty of space for a map of the places in Chidiock's poem. I've already drawn two of them!"

"Down at the bottom – *a family mansion looking out to sea*?"

"Yes! That's Tyneham."

"And the curvy line running from side to side across the base of the map – that must be the sea-coast. And then at the top, you've drawn Athelhampton, right in the middle."

"Yes, Little Elizabeth solved that clue, it's where *babe and babes of thine confine.*"

"And what's this wiggly line next to Athelhampton, running almost parallel to the sea?"

"That's the river Pydele! I forgot to write its name."

"And what's the wavy line running right across the middle?"

"That's the river Frome. I don't know whether any of the clues are on that, but it's roughly parallel to the Pydele and the sea, so it seemed logical to put it in."

"But you haven't put any other clues on here!"

"No." Anne lowered her eyes. "I couldn't think of any others, yet."

"I..." said Lizzie, hesitating, "I told Robert about all the clues, I hope that was alright?"

"Yes of course! The more heads the better!"

"He had an idea."

"Tell me!"

"It's for the one about the '*Symonds Castle*'. He once did some repairs for a man called Symonds, with his father."

"He seems to have done repairs for everyone!"

"That's because he's such a good mason," said Lizzie, blushing. "But we can't put it on the map yet, for 'twas a long time ago and he can't remember where it was, save that it's on the road to Dorchester."

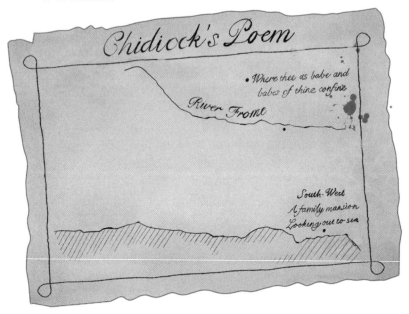

"That's strange, I've been that way many times and never saw a castle."

"I'll ask old Ma Melemouth, she's been to so many houses to deliver babies and treat ailments."

"And I'll try Master Bond. He seems to know all the big houses round here, I suppose because it's part of his job to negotiate with their owners when he needs to buy food for the house."

Lizzie stood up. "I mustn't stay too long, they'll miss me in the kitchen. But I'm wondering: even if we find out all the places, what might it mean?"

"The first line says '*when sun shines not so bright.*' I think that means when...if...Chidiock and

Henry get into trouble."

"Into trouble? You mean, because of their plotting?"

"Yes! That's when the poem will show us a way to help, once we've worked out where all these places are."

There came a sound of hooves on the flagstones of the courtyard. Lizzie jumped up and ran out of the door, and Anne barely had time to draw breath before she was back, saying, "William's gone! I saw him riding out through the Gatehouse! But the other strange man is still here, he came into the house with your father."

"Who is he?"

"I couldn't see his face under the rim of his hat."

Lizzie scurried off to help in the kitchen and Anne looked at the pile of kirtles, choosing one to change into, for her mother liked her to wear something smart when a visitor arrived. She laced it up, tied the bows on her shoes, checked that her hair was straight by looking at the reflection in the water in her bowl, and hurried downstairs to see who it was.

In the windowless Screens Passage, the great oaken door out to the courtyard was closed and the curtains across the doorways into the Great Hall were drawn shut to stop the draughts, so Anne could see almost nothing. She picked her way forward slowly, lest she trip on an uneven flagstone or on Gyb. She caught a whiff of the sea, and heard a strange metallic noise, like an old chain being pulled across the floor. As she peered through the murk she saw a dark figure – were those fronds of seaweed clinging to its three-pointed hat? Her mouth fell open and she crossed herself, whispering slowly, "Good Captain Heynes...is it thee, or a ghost?"

The figure burst out laughing, sweeping open the curtains, causing light from the Great Hall to flood into the passage. Wiping the last of the mud off its boot on to the iron scraper by the door, it bowed low and lifted off the hat, which Anne now saw was plumed with turquoise feathers. It looked up and said, "Good maid Anne, forgive the fright I gave thee! Ghost I am for the sheriffs and justices, for a spectre cannot be hanged, but for my old shipmates, I am very much alive. And my debt to Endy is still assigned to thee – my cutlass is ready when ye need it."

Anne stared at the figure's outrageous bright blue velvet and red breeches, thinking that they looked too clean and fresh, and too expensive, for a ghost. "But they said ye was drowned! Everyone said it. Nigh on a year ago, swept off the deck of thy own ship in a storm off Biscay!"

"That were a difficult time. Commissioners and sheriffs, a month or so after I drowned, they took all of my kind, Clinton Atkinson, Purser, Vaughan and other good captains, strung 'em up on the gibbet at Wapping."

"But... how did you know that was going to happen?"

The Captain's gold teeth glinted as his grin spread even wider. "I always gave good gifts to my Lord Hutton, and they came back with interest. He's the Queen's favourite, he hears everything, and knew what was coming. He gave me fair warning to scarper, and where better to hide than in Davy Jones' Locker?"

Anne now burst out laughing herself, and curtseyed low, glad that her dress went some way towards the sartorial standard set by the Captain.

"Then full welcome to Athelhampton in life again, good Captain and shipmate. And may I ask what brings you here, for I hear that the old business of smuggling is sore depleted?"

"'Tis too true, good Anne, the departure of so many fine men with a noose of Bridport hemp on their necks has dampened enthusiasm for the trade, though it creeps back slowly as greed conquers fear. And I must be more careful than most, lest unwelcome eyes realise that the storm in Biscay Bay was not so fierce that day. But a fine cargo of silks arrived a week back, more discreet and valuable than a shipload o' barrels, so I was not averse to helping out. I'm sending them to the merchants in Dorchester market in your uncle Henry's cart – all save a few bolts that Sir Nicholas has taken at a fair price to give to your good mother, and one taken by that Arundell lad."

Anne giggled, pleased at the thought that she might soon be wearing a dress made up from pirate silk, and amused that the noble William was not averse to a little contraband. "The weave will be all the finer for having escaped the excise!" Her face became more serious as she added: "And...why are you using Henry's cart?"

"I heard that he asked the ostlers to take it to Dorchester to give to his kinsman from Tyneham – so I offered them a few coins to pop my silk on the back. 'Tis much safer that way! 'Twould be dangerous for a dead man to take goods to a town where he was once well known."

Anne eyes widened in surprise at this news, but she couldn't think what it meant, and before she could ask more, the Captain bowed deep, the plume again brushing the floor. "And now, I must away. If ye need a cutlass to remove a head from its shoulders, ye will find me at the house of Mistress Munday in Corfe."

He swept away and as the curtains closed behind him, Anne raced to the kitchen, where she found Lizzie stirring an enormous pot of stew with a long wooden pole. She found another and started to help, saying breathlessly, "That strange man was Captain Heynes! He only pretended to drown."

"Alive? Are you sure? It might have been a ghost."

"His cutlass looked real enough! And he told me that a cart of Henry's is being sent to Dorchester market tomorrow, to be used by his kinsman."

"What for? Surely any relative of Henry's must be rich enough to have plenty of carts to carry fodder – and we know he doesn't approve of smuggling!"

"So, it must be something to do with the plot."

"But what?"

"I don't know, but I've decided to go to Dorchester tomorrow, to try and find out. I can go with Master Bond, he always goes to market to buy food for the cooks – and on the way, I can ask him about *Symonds Castle*."

"But who will you be looking for when you get there? That poor young shepherd's probably ill. So, that horrid Nathan will be the only person there from Tyneham that you'll know, and he's dangerous!"

Anne's heart began to pump so hard at this reminder of the attack on the cliffs that she had to stop stirring. She stood still for a moment to calm herself, lifted her head up straight and looked at Lizzie. "You're right, I have to look for him. And when I find him, I'll have to work out some way to deal with him."

ANNE OF ATHELHAMPTON

Chapter 6

Dorchester Market

"Do ye know the Symonds house?" Anne wore her cloak over her riding-kirtle, glad of its fur-lined hood in the cold of the bright morning as she set off for Dorchester market. Master Bond rode beside her, his chest resplendent in the Martyn family livery with the ape in its centre, embroidered on the fine fabric that befitted the man in charge of the Athelhampton household.

"Why yes, 'tis an old building on the back-road to Dorchester. We can go that way if ye wish, 'twill take but a few minutes more."

At Puddletown they turned onto a side road, and her companion said, "How is thy new mount? He looks most noble."

"He's already saved me," said Anne, without thinking. She blushed as she remembered that she needed to be discreet, quickly adding, "The way was slippery in the rain, and he kept balance perfectly!" thinking that was was a true, if incomplete, description of her trip to Tyneham.

They crossed a narrow bridge over a fast-flowing river, turned to ride beside it, and after a few minutes a large structure loomed ahead in the morning mist. Anne gripped her reins in excitement: here was the solution to one of the clues, right in front of her.

Tumble-down walls formed three sides of an enormous square; on the fourth was a thatched building as tall as Athelhampton, fallen stones strewn around and a cluster of birds tearing out straw from a hole in the roof. "It looks as though it's about to collapse!" she said, thinking as she spoke of the fourth line of the poem: '*the Symonds castle falls.*'

"Aye, and parts of it already have, for 'twas once a great castle, but much of it now lies in the river."

"Why didn't they repair such a fine building?"

"The earls who owned it lost their heads, and their estates, in the wars 'twixt York and Lancaster. Their families got the property back when old Henry, our good Queen's grandfather, came to the throne – but this place was already falling down and they never bothered to rebuild it."

Anne was barely listening to him, for she was thinking that Lizzie and Robert had been right – and now she knew the location of the *Symonds castle*, she could add it to the left-hand side of the map, just beside the Frome river.

As they rode towards the centre of Dorchester, Master Bond kept telling stories about the old wars. Anne started to yawn, despite the cold, almost wishing she'd never set him off by asking about the Symonds castle.

At last they reached a large field full of tethered horses and stationary wagons, with farmers loading and unloading goods. As Anne dismounted, she said: "Might we find the people from Tyneham here?"

"I never bother with them, they're rude and have nothing to sell. I buy fodder from Baron Dacre's farmers – he knows thy father, so they give me good prices. Come, I'll show ye."

Anne followed Master Bond into the busy market, and as he started buying some hay, she watched the farmers haggling over piles of corn and barrels of pitch, to see if she could spot Nathan. But there was no sign of him, and beyond the farmers' stalls, her eyes were drawn to a stand adorned with amber earrings, necklaces bearing red gems, and hair bands sparkling with a hint of gold.

She looked away quickly, for that wasn't what she'd come for. But Master Bond had followed her gaze and he said, "Ah, that stall is run by a Moor named Blanke – speak to him, he'll offer ye his best pieces, for his father became friends with thy ancestor, old Sir William, soon after he arrived from Africa."

The stallholder, who looked even older than the most ancient of the yeoman at Harvest Supper, leaned forward and said, "A fine silver bracelet for ye, young mistress?"

Anne pulled the bracelet onto her wrist, hoping that if she started trying things on, Master Bond would become bored with watching her and concentrate on buying fodder and supplies for the house, allowing her to give him the slip.

The jeweller put a necklace with sparkling green gems into her hands, saying, "Good mistress, a fine stone to catch the eye of thy sweetheart?"

An image of Anthony Floyer, a young man she'd once danced with, came into her mind. She started to bring the stones up to her neck before stopping abruptly and handing them back. "I've not seen him for a long time – he must now be promised to another."

"Then wear these, for ye is sure to catch the eye of a different suitor." He handed her a pair of sparkling pearl earrings.

"Let me try." Looking at them brought an image of her Grandma's wonderful pearl necklace into her mind, and on impulse she said: "I'm sorry, good Master Blanke. Some other pearls that were promised to me have been lost, and I've just decided that I won't buy any jewels, nor accept any as a gift, until I get them back."

Blanke bowed again. "I wish ye luck in the search for them."

Anne turned to check on Master Bond and saw that he was now too engrossed in buying pewter plates to see what she was doing. She strode away swiftly, passing bolts of fine Flemish silk spread out like a rainbow which she guessed had come from Captain Heynes, and hurried back to the crowded area round the farmers' stalls.

As she arrived there, she glimpsed a figure stepping swiftly away from her line of sight. She found herself trembling – was she was being watched by Nathan, even as she searched for him? She slipped in among a large group of people, hoping this would make it easier to see without being seen.

The people around her were shouting loudly, their fists raised and faces red with anger:

"How can there be none left?"

"I need pitch for my roof!"

"How can I repair my boat without pitch?"

"Ye cannot have sold out so soon."

She caught her breath as she spotted the figure who didn't want to be seen by her. This time, she saw more: it was a man with a good head of hair, so it couldn't be Nathan. Determined to find out who it was, she circled round, ducking her head below the level of the crowd, so as to come behind him unawares. As she came through a group of shepherds she saw him, just three steps away, his back turned as he stared to where she had been. He wore livery emblazoned with three birds in dark grey on a silver background – the Tregonwell choughs!

She inhaled sharply as she realised it was Walter Bearde, servant to her unpleasant cousin Young John. Why was he here? He and his master had done terrible things in the past and she'd wished she would never see either of them again, but here he was, following her. She slid away, and moved into another dense group of angry men, squashing in among them so that he would not see her.

In the midst of the melee was a small man, standing with his hands on a pile of black-stained, tarry barrels as he shouted: "I told you, no!"

"You have half a dozen left, you can sell me just one!"

"You can't have them," said the small man, his face reddening, "I've been promised a good price, more than you could ever pay. They'll be collected by the purchaser soon. You should have come earlier!"

Puzzled by this exchange, but with Walter off her trail for a moment and still seeing no sign of Nathan,

Anne walked towards a nearby tavern, remembering her father saying that deals were often closed over a tankard or two of ale. Its wide open door was surmounted by two torches blazing in broad daylight to attract customers, while at ground level a large board announced a competition to guess the weight of a sow.

She spied Walter in the distance coming towards her and moved behind the board. He was looking round as he approached but did not peer behind the sign, instead plunging into the interior of the inn. She wondered whether to wait and see whether Nathan appeared, or to go and search in the large field fifty paces away beyond the old Roman city walls, where farmers loaded their purchases onto carriages and carts.

'I'll watch five more people go in or out, and if he's not among them, then I'll go to the carts,' she decided. Two yeomen came out almost at once, tripping on their own feet and clapping one another on the back, followed by two gentlemen talking excitedly – but neither was her target. She waited for what seemed forever, but was probably another two minutes, and the old Moor walked over. Five people, and no sign of that sinister bald head.

She set off for the gap in the ruined city walls that led to the carriage area, hurrying so much that she almost fell over the two drunken yeomen who were seated on the fallen stones just at the point where everyone was trying to squeeze through.

Once past the obstacle, she scanned the vast field of carts, horses and carriages, and her palms went moist as she saw a group of five wagons standing apart from all others in a nearby corner of the field. The sides of one were emblazoned with Henry's livery and the other four carried the distinctive arms she'd seen on that terrifying trip to Tyneham: three birds and a horse. Two of the carts were already fully laden with straw and a group of men was rolling barrels of pitch up a plank onto a third.

"Come on, Nathan, work a bit harder!" came a cry, and Anne felt a stab of fear as she saw her former assailant rolling a barrel towards the ramp. He had a crude bandage on one arm and walked with a limp, which she guessed must be a result of Bayard's charge.

"We need more," said a white-haired, well-dressed old man standing nearby.

'This,' thought Anne, 'must be Nathan's master!'

The grating voice of Nathan came across the field: "I've bought all the pitch in the market, bar the final six casks, the seller of those is gouging me. He claims they are the only ones left in all Dorsetshire. There'll be new supplies at Mylton market two weeks hence, they're sure to be cheaper."

"Two weeks!" Anne could hear the anger in the white-haired man's voice as he replied. "The weather will change before then, the ships will go and the chance will be lost. Henry has enough gold, just pay what you're asked."

Anne pushed her lips hard together to suppress her instinct to make an angry cry. There were already almost a score of barrels here, and now they would buy six more! No farmer needed so much pitch to repair his roofs or his ponds. Set a flame to it and it burns hot and hard, and that must be what they planned, whether to light a beacon for approaching ships or to burn down Dorchester – she remembered William talking of a plot to set fire to buildings. Whatever they wanted to do, with all that pitch it must be evil.

She had intended simply to gather intelligence on this trip and then go home and make a plan. However, the talk of the imminent change in weather suggested that urgent action was needed. But how could she, all alone, do anything to stop these villains from their devil's work?

For a moment she regretted not asking Captain Heynes to bring his cutlass and be ready to help. Then a sliver of hope came to her: even if the good Captain was beside her now, he would not single-handedly attack the ten or more ruffians rolling that pitch onto the wagons – rather, he would find some indirect weapon. She tried to put herself into his mind and as she looked around, she found herself formulating a strategy.

Bayard was tethered with other horses on the far side of the field. She took a circuitous route to reach him, keeping well away from the five wagons and the men around them, but hurrying, for she had no idea how long they would take to get the rest of the pitch. She gave the lad guarding the horses a ha'penny and told him to tell Master Bond that she'd felt tired and gone home early.

She took out from her saddlebag a fraying old blanket borrowed from the stables and arranged it carefully to cover Bayard's magnificent mane and his tell-tale birthmark. She pulled her hood over her head, put an old leather belt round her waist, and picked up a handful of dark muck from the ground, which she smeared on her fine new leather boots and her cheekbones, before rubbing the remainder over both hands. The smell was disgusting and she didn't want to think about what was in it, but she had no time for niceties and the muck made her look more like a village lad than the young lady of a great Dorsetshire house.

She undid the halter, mounted Bayard, and rode to the side of the tavern. There came a rumble of wood on stone and she saw Nathan and his fellows rolling six casks, which must be the extra ones they had just bought from the market. They passed far closer to her than she had intended, and she prayed that her hood, the dirt and the old blanket were sufficient disguise. As they went through the gap in the city wall in the direction of the wagons she clenched her fists as she realised that it would not take long to load the extra barrels; once that was done, Nathan and his cronies would be gone. She had to act now or abandon any chance of stopping the plot.

She walked Bayard right up to the entrance of the inn, oblivious to the cries of objection from those trying to enter, not caring whether Walter or Master Bond was there, for now she was determined to execute her plan come what may. She reached up and seized the first of the two torches from above the door in her left hand and the second in her right. Holding them aloft, she urged Bayard forward. He broke into a fast trot, baying, and people jumped aside as she came between the old Roman stones and

raced up to the nearest of the wagons.

Suddenly everyone was shouting, men were racing up and trying to grab her, and she felt her foot almost hauled out of the stirrup. Bayard moved on regardless, and Anne leaned forward and hurled the first torch onto the barrels.

With neither hand on the reins and Bayard trotting so fast it seemed like a gallop, the action unbalanced her and she would have fallen off, had he not leaned hard over to that side so she could haul herself back upright with her free hand.

She looked back over her shoulder at the wagons and saw that the torch had been extinguished. Throwing it on the barrels had been a mistake, for their solid oak would not catch light easily. She steadied herself to try again and gasped as she saw a group of ruffians racing towards her, brandishing pitchforks and staves; from the corner of her eye, she saw Walter standing nearby, not joining in but with his hands on his hips as though watching a show, the old Moor next to him.

Anne dug in her spurs and Bayard leapt forward towards the men. Most of them jumped aside but Nathan stood his ground, raising the pitchfork to strike her face full on. She screamed out loud at the thought of the searing pain but Bayard did not slow, instead swerving to the side at the last moment to avoid the deadly points, with his rear flank catching Nathan full on.

Then they were right beside the wagons and this time Anne plunged the remaining torch into the dry hay. This caught light immediately in great waves of flame, which in barely a moment engulfed the nearest barrels of pitch. She saw that Nathan was on the ground but the other men were trying to encircle her by bringing up two big shire-horses. Bayard let out a great trumpeting note and the other animals broke from their masters and fled.

Bayard surged forward, away from the wagons, unbidden by Anne, who clung on to stay in the saddle even as the acceleration tore away the old blanket, which fell to the ground. She felt heat hitting her from behind like the wind in a storm and then there came a second and a third shock, each hotter and stronger than before. She glanced back and let out a shout of triumph as she saw that the pitch was exploding uncontrollably as barrel after barrel ignited and the fire spread among the close-packed wagons, with men scattering in all directions.

Bayard sped on and away and the cries and the heat were left far behind.

ANNE OF ATHELHAMPTON

Chapter 7
Plot and Counter Plot

Anne stood beside Robert, looking at the fire-damaged wagon in a corner of the back courtyard.

"It must have arrived very early," she said. "It wasn't here last night."

"One of the Sheriff's men delivered it soon after dawn," said Robert, running his eyes carefully across the charred remnants of the timber-work. "He said the Justices have finally finished examining it – they wanted evidence to confirm their suspicions that Nathan and his master were involved with Scarface." Anne started fidgeting anxiously. "Did they find anything? It might lead them back to Henry and Chidiock."

"No, it was too badly burnt."

"That's a relief. Though I wouldn't have minded if Nathan had been arrested." There was a creaking sound from the old gate in the corner of the courtyard and over the mason's shoulder, Anne saw Eliza and Henry coming through it, deep in conversation.

"The Sheriff's man also told me," added Robert, smiling, "that everyone thinks a village boy threw the torches."

Anne was smiling as well. "So there was no mention of a girl?"

"Nay, ye need have no fear. And I asked him whether the Sheriff knew of any ships landing along the old smuggling bays, and he said no. So, ye has succeeded – the plot has been stopped."

"Thank goodness!"

Anne caught Eliza's gaze, and saw there was dampness round her sister's eyes. "What's wrong?" she asked, guessing that it might be something to do with the plot.

"I...don't want to talk about it now. Maybe I'll tell you later."

Henry had joined Robert in inspecting the cart, saying: "I hear ye are soon to the end of thy apprenticeship, and will become a master mason."

"Aye, 'twill be soon now."

"Then ye will need a wagon, so I thought to gift this to ye. I have carts a-plenty at home, and have no need of this one. Ye will need to replace all these burnt timbers, of course."

"'Tis uncommon generous. The wheels and frame are sound, that is what matters, and I accept with thanks."

"Will it take long to repair?"

"Not too long, 'twill be ready in time for my first job. I need to fetch stones from one of the ruined churches in the lost villages; they are no use where they are, but will look fine in the new wall I have promised Sir Nicholas."

"At least," said Eliza, "some good will have come out of this sorry affair." She took Anne's arm, saying, "May I talk with you for a few minutes?"

The two sisters left Henry and Robert with the cart and went into the kitchen garden, and as they strolled between the herbs, Anne said, "What did you mean, about a sorry affair?"

"Henry gave Chidiock some gold, and let him use the wagon, for some bad venture. But it all went wrong."

Anne took a deep breath. She wanted to find out as much as she could, and to do that, would have to reveal some of what she had been doing. She said, "Involving ships, landing on the coast?"

Eliza stopped, and looked her sister direct in the eyes. "How did you know that?"

"I was out for a ride, I went to Tyneham, and spoke with some servants."

"Then you know as much as I."

"Thank goodness 'tis all now finished!"

"I wish that were true. But Henry says the venture with the ships was just the first step in a much bigger plan, the idea was to demonstrate power and bring support, but even without that they will move on to the next stage. To finance that, Chidiock has asked for more gold." Anne's hands went chill, as she remembered how William had said that the plan with the ships was part of a treacherous plot to put Mary on the throne, because she supported the old religion.

Eliza continued: "I told Henry he must not do it, but he insisted that giving away his gold was his own business and of no concern to a wife. He was harsh with me, worse than he's ever been before."

"You've been crying, and no wonder!" said Anne, and she put her arms around her sister and hugged her, "Of course it is thy business if he does such a thing. And I don't understand how Henry can speak that way to you – the two of you always seem so happy together."

"It's...something that you will learn, if you ever marry. Things are wonderful to begin with, and then they change. He's not trying to hurt me, it's just that he's so deep in his own schemes, he thinks what he's doing must be for the best and pays less attention to what I say."

Anne nodded in sympathy, and said, "Do you know when Henry is to provide this gold?"

"A week from today. It will be delivered to Chidiock and Jane's house at Almer."

"Mother! Aunt Anne! Aunt Anne!" On the opposite side of the kitchen garden, Little Elizabeth and her small siblings Janie, Marie and Francis appeared, racing towards them, hand in hand. Anne saw that her opportunity would be gone in a moment, so she said quickly, "Was there anything else that Henry told you?"

"He said there will be much more gold than before. 'Twill be every last coin that he has left, save the few he must keep for the farm. That's all he would say."

The children arrived, shouting again, "Mother, Aunt Anne!"

Anne said, "But I am too young to be called Aunt!" and they started to dance around her and Eliza, chanting, "*Humpty Dumpty sat on a wall*," and holding hands as they went round and round, and then they threw themselves on the ground, shouting, "*...had a great fall!*"

Anne could not stop herself from bursting out laughing, and Eliza smiled as she said, "Now, children, those clothes will be filthy! Pick yourselves up and let's go and eat the midday meal."

"Yes mother!" said Little Elizabeth, "And afterwards please can we see Lizzie, everyone's saying that she and Robert are getting betrothed, we want to pick some flowers and give them to her!"

Anne waved at the children as Eliza took them off to eat, and retraced her steps to the back courtyard, where Robert was starting to repair the cart, Lizzie beside him holding a wicker laundry-basket. She took the maidservant's free hand and said, "I've heard your betrothal's official! That's wonderful!"

"Yes," said Lizzie, "we can announce it properly, now that Robert's about to become a master mason. It's especially nice that it's happening just after you've sorted out all the troubles with Chidiock and Henry!"

Anne's shoulders fell. "I'm afraid they are moving on to the next stage in their plot! Eliza just told me about it. Henry is providing lots of gold for it."

Lizzie stared at her, and Robert looked up from his work and said, "What is it?"

Anne hesitated before she replied: "I don't know the details, but it's something dangerous to do with politics."

"Where is the gold?" said Lizzie.

"He's sending it to Chidiock and Jane's house at Almer, a week from today," said Anne, "so I had an idea..."

"What kind of idea?" said Lizzie.

"I...I wondered, whether we could somehow take it."

"You mean steal it?" said Robert.

"Not steal it," said Anne. "We'd just hide it somewhere, so it couldn't be used in the plot!"

"But how would we do that?" said Lizzie, looking at Robert. "Could we put it in thy cart?"

"Gold is heavy," said Robert, "anything more than a couple of bags would be too much, even with the new timbers I'm putting on."

"Then we'll have to find another solution, even if we have to bury it in a field at night!" said Anne. "I'll go and visit Jane at Almer on the day it gets delivered, see where it gets put, and then we can make a plan."

"But will Jane want to see you?" asked Lizzie. "I thought you two were having a row."

Anne squeezed her fingers into her palms, uncomfortable at being reminded of this. "We have been," she said slowly, "and I want to end that, but I'm not sure how to do it."

Master Bond appeared through a doorway, and Lizzie started shuffling the clothes in her basket, saying loudly, "I must get these smocks into the boiling-pot." She turned to hurry away to the laundry, while Robert went off to find wood to repair the wagon.

Anne went in search of her mother and found her in the Screens Passage, watching as two of the maids adjusted the position of a new tapestry.

"Mother..." she started, swallowing hard as she tried to pluck up courage to ask for help in contacting Jane, but realised that the servants were in earshot and instead said, "...will there be a party for Robert and Lizzie's betrothal?"

"Yes, I'm planning it now. I'm going to have new dresses made up for you and all your sisters, using some excellent silks that your father has bought. You will be the first to choose." The maids finished their work, curtseyed, and went away, and the Lady Margaret continued, "My mother is most anxious that you have this, to wear to the party." She drew from her pocket a little box covered in exquisite blue velvet, and opened it to reveal a gold necklace with a beautiful opal.

Anne put her hand out and then let it slump back to her side. Her maternal grandmother, Joan Wadham, now very old indeed, regularly gave her granddaughters gifts of jewellery. But she could not accept this without breaking the resolution she had made in the market. "I...that's so kind of Grandmother Joan! But I have so much jewellery already. It seems unfair to take more from her."

"You shouldn't worry. My mother is very wealthy, she likes to give things away, she's even asked my brother Nicholas use her money to create a new college for the university at Oxford."

"Then...might this be given as a present to Lizzie, to mark her betrothal?"

The Lady Margaret was silent for a moment, and then said, "'Twould be a most exceptional gift for a maidservant! But 'tis such a kind thought, and Lizzie is almost like another sister to thee. So, let us do it."

Anne pushed the little box into her pocket and took a deep breath, as she thought how to phrase the next thing she had to say. "Mother, Jane and I have been arguing, but I want to make up with her. I'm planning to ride over to Almer to see her. I'll write her a letter to go in the next package you send over to her, and would you write to her yourself, saying that I want to be friends again?"

"I knew you two were having a fight, and I didn't know how to end it, so it's lovely that you go to her, rather than waiting for her to come here – that shows you're making a real effort. And, of course I'll write! Anne broke into a broad smile. "Thank you!"

"You should go before Thursday of next week, for that's when she's closing up her house to come and stay here for a couple of months. It's miserable for her to be all alone, now that Chidiock has a new job and will be away until summer."

"If she's coming for several weeks, she'll be bringing lots of things. So I'll ride over there the day before she arrives and see whether she needs any help with packing." As Anne said this, she was thinking: that means I'll be there on the very day that the gold arrives.

Chapter 8
Young John

"From Young John?" Anne didn't know whether her eyes or her mouth had opened wider, as she took the letter from the hands of Master Bond. She'd thought he was bringing her a message from Jane about arrangements for her trip to Almer, which was now only two days away.

"It arrived late last night, Mistress Anne. Ye had already retired to your room, I knew ye was tired and I thought ye would be sound abed, so I waited till this morning. I hope that was correct."

Anne nodded her thanks and closed her bedroom door. She looked at the three choughs on the seal and felt herself quivering as she remembered how so often that had signalled a letter from her dear Grandma, the Lady Elizabeth. But now, it meant nothing more than a message from her horrible cousin. Rather than breaking the seal neatly, she bought it down hard on the edge of her oak chest so that it shattered into lots of small pieces. What a travesty that he had the legal right to the same crest!

She opened the letter. "*My dear cousin Anne.*" How dare he call me 'dear', she thought, just as there came a knock on the door.

Lizzie entered, carrying a broomstick as though

to clean, but Anne burst into laughter at once. "Lizzie! I know you too well. You saw Master Bond come in here, and came to find out what is going on!" Lizzie blushed and nodded, and Anne continued, smiling, "And that's just as well, for I have this strange letter from my cousin, and I need to share it with thee!"

"Thy cousin? Young John? His servant Walter was watching you in Dorchester and now he's writing to you. I wonder why he's suddenly interested in you again."

"Whatever he wants, it'll be to help him, not me. Sit down and I'll read to both of us."

"*It may seem strange that I write after all that has happened, but I have been poorly these last times and now...,*" Anne paused and took a deep breath, "*...I have not long before I meet my Maker.*"

"Even though he is not yet an old man," said Lizzie.

"Maybe it's a judgement from God for the bad things he has done!"

"Do you feel glad?"

"I'm trying not to, though I don't feel sad, of course!"

"What does he say next?"

"*As my time approaches, I have decided that I wish to ask thy forgiveness for the wrongs that I have committed against thee.*" Anne paused and looked at Lizzie. "I don't want to forgive him. He did such terrible things."

"But we are meant to be forgiving, aren't we? That's what the good Vicar Gange says it tells us in the Bible."

"Yes, I know," said Anne, her voice almost like a growl. "So, I suppose I shall have to forgive him." She sat silent for a moment before picking up the letter again. "He goes on: *There is one wrong for which I can still make amends. Our grandmother, before she died, asked me to give some fine pearls to you.* Then he admits that he stole them!" She squeezed her hands into fists, crushing the sides of the letter, and continued, "Listen to this: *I did not do as she asked, instead I hid them. And now, I wish to give them to you and fulfil her command.*"

"So did he send the pearls with this letter?"

"No, it's not as simple as that. He says, *I am keeping them safe for you. Please come to see me as soon as you can, and I will restore them to you. My repentance is a private matter between us so please come alone.*" Anne looked up, frowning, and said, "I don't believe this is about forgiveness, I'm sure he has some evil intent. That's his way."

"I think you're right, but those pearls are wonderful, I remember them! And what's more important, your Grandma intended them for you!" Anne nodded, and stared back down at the letter, her own brow creased, and she spoke slowly. "There is some trick here, but I have to go and fetch them. And when I'm there, I may find some clues to his plans. Bayard can bear me away quickly if he tries to do something bad."

"To Mylton Abbey," said Anne, and Bayard turned towards the village of Tolpuddle. Children were splashing one another with water from the pump in the warmth of the sun, but she felt a lump in her throat as the sound of the blacksmith's hammer reminded her of the time when she used to ride this way every week to see her Grandma. Her usual route led up a steep and little-used short-cut, where she found a great bough lying across the track, forcing her to ease Bayard through the bushes to reach the open road that ran the last few miles into Mylton. Approaching the gates of what she would always think of as the Lady Elizabeth's home, she squeezed her hands tight around the reins as she thought of Young John now living there.

She dismounted and a footman opened the great entrance door. A large picture of Queen Elizabeth in exquisite lacework stared down regally from above the stairs, usurping the spot where the portrait of Grandma's youthful beauty used to hang.

"'Tis a fine work, Mistress Anne!"

Anne turned abruptly, surprised at being addressed by name, and started to reply. "I…" She stopped, swallowing hard and unable to say anything, as she looked into the eyes of Anthony Floyer.

He had grown taller than she remembered from their first meeting a year or so before, his fair hair well kempt above a slim face with clear brown eyes. She had liked him then, and had been thankful for the extraordinary help he had offered her in a moment of crisis. But what was he doing in the house of her unscrupulous cousin, where any activity must be regarded with suspicion? There was silence for several moments, until at last she was able to say,

"My Lord Floyer…the painting is fine, but na'er so fine as the one of my Grandma that it replaces."

"Please, you should say Anthony. And I...I remember that portrait, it was indeed beautiful…"

"May I ask," Anne said sharply, frowning, "what brings you here, to the house of my cousin?"

"There is some legal work, a codicil to his will. 'Twas urgent, with so little time left. 'Tis done now."

"You do that for a man such as Young John?"

Anthony coughed, and said, "I had to come here, as an articled clerk I must do what my principal requires. 'Twas not my own choice! I would never wish to help a man who did you great harm."

Anne's face relaxed. "That is how I remember you from before, when you tried to protect me from him – and when we danced together at my sister's betrothal party!"

"What a wonderful day!"

"And where do you live now?"

"I am still in Exeter, with my good mother."

"Surely, you must have a bride?"

"None has caught my fancy. And might I ask much the same of you?"

"You might, and I would reply just as you did," said Anne, laughing as she spoke, and as Anthony joined in, she decided he was even nicer than when she had first met him. For a moment, she thought how fine it would be to see him again and have him for her suitor, and then she remembered the ride from Athelhampton with the wind in her hair and the sun on her face, and she thought, 'but I am still too young to marry.'

She heard a cough, and realised that the footman

was there. "Mistress Anne, my master begs your presence."

Anne smiled again at Anthony, saying, "I must take my leave. 'Twas a great pleasure to see you again."

"The pleasure was mine."

She curtseyed, and he bowed, and she turned away to follow the footman.

She was taken along a long corridor with tall tapestries hanging on the wall, where her eye was drawn to small holes and fraying edges. The new owner of Mylton Abbey clearly did not have a mouser as good as Gyb and she smiled for a moment, until she remembered that her mother always said not to enjoy the misfortunes of others, whoever they were.

They approached the doors that led into the great chamber, where the ancient statues of King Athelstan and his Queen stood. She knew this had been her Grandma's favourite room, and she squeezed her lips together as she saw a man lying on a couch between the royal figures, usurping the place where the old lady always used to welcome visitors. It was Young John.

"Welcome, good cousin," he said, his face wan, his hands thin and his voice low, and it seemed to Anne as though each word was spoken with an effort that cost him an hour of his life. "I thank God that you are here, for little time is left to me, and I have words long wished to say to you."

"I have come as you asked, cousin," said Anne, remembering the deep curtsies she had made to him before, but this time taking taking the folds of her kirtle and dipping her knees barely a few inches.

"I have done you wrong, and I cannot go to meet Our Lord until I have your forgiveness. I gave you a gift, with ill intent. I pressed suit for your hand, not from love nor respect, but from mercenary motive. I fought with your father, and sought disrepute on your house."

"You did great wrong, not just to me, but to our dear Grandma." Anne spoke slowly and deliberately, trying to use the tone that her mother used when speaking on the most serious matters. "For what you did to Grandma, you must look to God for forgiveness." She paused, tempted to say 'and that is also the only way to find solace for your crimes against me,' and then turn her heel and walk away without waiting for the pearls. But she remembered her discussion with Lizzie, and with a feeling of nausea in her stomach, she said, "For what you did to me, I offer you my forgiveness."

"I thank you, good Mistress Anne. And now, I have an important thing to do. Pray, open the chest there, by the wall. Here is the key."

Anne took the great iron key from a trembling hand, and went over to the oaken chest. It was newly carved by a master who had made swirling shapes like waves that twined together, and had a dark iron plate with a large keyhole. She put the key in and turned it, and tried to lift the lid, thinking for a moment that she had not fully unlocked it, until she realised that the weight was greater than any she had opened before.

"There are fabrics, in red and gold, should I lift those out?"

"Nay, good Anne, place those to the left side, and look to what you find underneath."

"There are just wooden planks at the bottom of the chest."

"You will see a carving of a sea-monster inside the lid. Find the place on the planks nearest to that, and press down as hard as ye may."

Anne put her hand as she was bid, and pressed. Nothing happened, so she pressed harder, and at last the downward pressure caused the opposite side of a plank to lift. She looked inside the cavity that had been revealed and said, "There is a bag of grey velvet."

"Pray bring it here and open it."

Anne undid the drawstring of the bag and gently pulled out a gleaming white necklace. She stood motionless, clasping the jewels softly as though holding the hand of a young child. At last she whispered, "They reflect a wonderful soft light, and yet at the same time, I can almost see right through them." She was reminded of when she had been a young girl sitting and reading with her Grandma, and of the first time the old lady had met Endy, in this very room, and she felt surrounded by a warm glow.

She became aware that Young John was staring straight at her, and she carefully returned the pearls to the bag and hooked it to her waistband. "Grandma told me that they were given to her by the Queen, in the days when she went to Court in London with old Sir John."

"Before she died, our Grandma asked me to give them to you. With all your sisters married, she wanted you to have them to wear at your wedding."

Anne returned Young John's stare. "Then you should have done as she asked!" she said, astonished by her own boldness.

"You should have learnt not to be rude when you were younger!" cried Young John, half sitting up as his voice gained strength. "Be careful, lest I ask you to return those pearls to me!"

Anne's voice also rose. "They are not yours, but if that's what you want, then I will give them to you," and she put her hands to her belt to unhitch the pouch. "The only reason I want them is that they remind me of Grandma and her love, but that memory is there with or without a few stones!"

Her cousin sank back on his couch and spoke in a small, whining voice, "Nay, they are yours, you should keep them, I want you to have them, I want that very much." His eyes closed, and all Anne could hear was a faint sound of breathing. She waited, counting the exhalations, but he lay still. She turned and started to walk away.

Suddenly, Young John spoke again. "Have you not the politeness to thank me for such a valuable gift?"

Anne turned back to him, hands on her hips. "How dare you!" she cried. "Those pearls were bequeathed to me by Grandma, and you stole them! Giving them back to me is no gift and demands no thanks!"

She swung round and strode away down the length of the great room, determined to give him no chance to say more. Just before she reached the doors at the end, she glanced through an open hatchway to the side, and for a moment she caught a fleeting glance of a familiar figure – could that be the horrid Walter? Before she could look closer, it was gone, and the footman was already beckoning her out to the hallway.

The warmth of the morning had turned to a midday heat, and the final part of the journey took her past the fields grazed by sheep where there were no trees for shade. As she rode back into the courtyard at Athelhampton, she felt hot in her woollen kirtle, and was looking forward to a tankard of small beer.

As she hurried into the Screens Passage, heading for the parlour where the ale was kept in a big barrel, something brushed against her leg. She bent down to stroke Gyb and hearing the click of a stick on the stone floor, she looked up to see the cat's owner, Ma Melemouth. The crone's back was curved with age, but within her wrinkled face, her eyes were bright as she looked at Anne and said: "Ye have had a good ride today?"

"Yes, I…I went to Mylton Abbey. Young John sent me a letter, he asked me to go and see him."

"Did he give ye something?"

"Yes…" Anne hesitated, and the pearls, hidden deep on her waistband under her riding-kirtle, somehow seemed to have increased in weight as though they were a great burden. "He was very ill…he said he wanted to give me Grandma's pearls before he died, he confessed that he should have given them to me sooner."

Anne felt Ma Melemouth's eyes looking deep into her. "They are thy pearls, and 'tis good that ye have them. But Young John acts only to hurt and destroy. He may be close to death, he may have used fair words, but he is falser than vows made in wine. This is a gift that spells danger for thee."

Anne found herself unable to say anything, and

the crone leaned closer to her and said, "Thy grandma was the strongest lady I ever knew, she saw off her enemies, and now ye must do the same. Ye have the memory of Endy to draw on when ye need strength."

Chapter 9

The Privy at Almer

"Such a lovely embrace!" The hug was so tight that Anne could see every strand of Jane's auburn hair and feel every heartbeat.

"I want to make up for being so distant at Harvest Supper. 'Tis so kind of you to ride all the way over to Almer to help with my packing." Jane took a step back, beaming, her wonderful cat-green eyes looking straight into Anne's.

Anne returned her sister's smile. "'Tis wonderful to see thee, on Bayard the journey is as nothing, I was so sad that we'd been arguing and I wanted to see you and be happy together."

"That's just how I feel as well! Come, let us sit outside, 'tis a fine day."

They sat under an old oak tree and a maidservant brought them small beer. "The church looks old, its yews must have been planted a hundred years ago. But thy house looks brand new, you must be so glad."

"Yes, 'twas barely finished when we moved in, and has so many modern things, a chimney that draws perfectly – and even a privy at the back," said Jane, giggling. "But tell me, what is happening at Athelhampton? I heard that William Arundell came to visit thee! Is he a serious suitor?"

"Nay, we had a fine talk, but it came to nothing."

"Don't be downhearted! 'Tis best to end these romances quickly, if they feel wrong – you are too young to remember the Viscount Bindon, who paid suit to Frances, but 'tis a story worth knowing. She rejected him, despite his high title, and she was right! He went mad, and now dresses as a monk and beats his servants."

Anne squeezed her hands together in excitement, as she realised this was the man in a white habit at the bridge over the Frome on the Tyneham road – solving another of the clues in Chidiock's poem, the *Lord who wears the monkish robes.*

Out loud, she just said, "I wasn't really upset about William – I'm still much too young to marry."

"Unlike Lizzie! Isn't it wonderful that she and Robert are to be betrothed! And I hear that Father bought some fine Huguenot silk for new kirtles, which we can wear to the party."

Anne smiled. "Yes, he got it from the good Captain Heynes."

Jane's beautiful deep green eyes widened. "Surely, God rest his soul, that villain departed this world off Biscay last year?"

"He has managed to swim home to Dorsetshire, with many bolts of good fabric and none of them even a little bit wet! But, tell me of thy news. I heard that Chidiock has a new appointment."

"He's been given his own Company in the yeomanry by his commander, Sir Christopher."

"Isn't that the same man who is renting this house to you?"

"Yes, and he said that we can buy it from him –

with this new job, it will only take a year or two to save enough money."

Anne felt herself starting to shiver, at the thought that if Chidiock was caught plotting, he would be arrested and have no chance to earn money. But out loud she said, "You should be really proud of Chidiock."

"'Tis wonderful to be promoted. But it means he spends much more time at Court."

"That is sad for thee, to be here without him."

Jane waited for a moment before replying, and lowered her voice. "There is something worse. I fell in love with Chidiock because he is such a gentle and kind man – and because we both believe in the old religion. But something has changed."

"The laws," said Anne, "are much tighter than they were. 'Tis more dangerous to have a priest."

"Yes, that's why I insisted Father Ballard be sent away from here, and he left two months ago. But that's not what I mean."

"What else is different?"

"Chidiock has gone much further than simply wanting to practice the old religion for himself. He has become involved in politics. It's a kind of obsession. He says that because Mary stands for the old religion, he wants..." and here Jane's voice dropped to a whisper, "he wants her to become Queen of England!"

Anne had guessed this already from what William and Eliza had said, but hearing it so clearly from Jane sent a feeling through her like an icy spike. "Mary in place of Elizabeth? But that is high treason!"

Jane nodded, and said, "I used to feel that you were against my religion – I was almost as angry as Chidiock when you didn't go to Mass at Yuletide. But now, I see that you just want to keep us all safe, and well away from politics and plots."

Anne put her arms around Jane, her eyes damp at the thought of her sister bearing the terrible secret of the plot alone. But now it was shared, and she felt her sadness ebbing as they hugged and she heard the familiar sounds of thrushes singing in the churchyard and earth churning through the blades of a plough.

There came the noise of wheels on stone, and Anne gently eased herself free and looked round. A flat wagon drawn by four large horses was rolling slowly up the track and round towards the back of the house. She looked at the cart and saw the arms of the Brunes on the side.

"That's from Henry and Eliza?" she asked.

"Yes," said Jane, "They have spare fodder, and are sending some to help the farmer here."

Anne began to wonder how she could watch it being unloaded without being seen, but was distracted by her sister, who was clearly in the mood for more confidences.

"Although we have sent Father Ballard away from here, my dear Chidiock still sees him regularly in London, and not just for the sacraments. They seem to be getting more closely involved."

"What do you mean?"

"I will read you some of his letters." Jane withdrew some letters from a pocket by her heart. "This one is from two months ago: *I went for a wonderful ride on Hampstead Heath this morning at first light, there is the most beautiful view towards St Paul's.* It goes on about other enjoyable activities. And this one is from a few weeks ago: *Today after the troop parades in front of Sir Christopher, he came up to me and said how smart my Yeomen looked. I had dinner with Farther Ballard and he congratulated me on getting such a good report from the Commander.*"

"But those all seem fine!"

"Yes," said Jane, her brow furrowed, "but listen to this one, from just a few days ago: *Yesterday, after a good ride to Chelsea and back, I had dinner with Father Ballard at the lodgings of a fine man, Anthony Babington, and we talked at great length about Mary.*"

Anne felt her heart beating faster. This sounded like the very plotting that she had promised herself to save Chidiock from. A cloud passed briefly across the sun and an old man in a ragged and patched jerkin walked across the churchyard, as she waited to see whether there would be more confidences about Babington, but there was nothing, so she stood up and said, "Come, show me round your fine modern house, I should like to see everything you have. I might even use the privy, though I have never tried one before!"

"Yes," said Jane, starting to smile, "I will show you everything, starting with that!" and she took Anne's hand and led her towards the house.

Following her sister's directions to the privy, Anne climbed a broad staircase to a landing on the top floor. To the left, a passage disappeared into a dark attic, to the right a narrow servants' stair led down, and ahead of her a rough plank door stood half ajar. She went through this and found a small wooden room, barely large enough for one person and lit only by some narrow louvres near the ceiling. There was an oak seat, which had a hole in the middle, and peering through it, Anne found herself looking down at a pile of straw on the ground below. She realised that the room was like a wooden box, attached to the back of the house and projecting out over the rear courtyard. She guessed that the straw would be removed once it became heavily soiled.

Very modern, thought Anne, and was just about to adjust her kirtle and skirts to use the privy, when she realised that by crouching down and bringing her head close to the seat, she could look through the hole and see most of the courtyard. There were two heavily-laden carts, which she guessed held all the things Jane was taking to Athelhampton, and beyond them was the wagon with the Brune arms that she had seen arriving a few minutes before.

Three men in Brune livery were arguing; they clearly didn't realise that the modern device of a privy allowed someone to watch and listen, and they did not look up.

"Why can't we just leave this stuff for someone else to unload?" grumbled a tall thin man. "It's uncommon heavy and we already had to load it up this morning."

"Just do what ye're paid for," said a short man, who seemed to be in charge. "Orders are to move it to that shed, so we move it."

A crazy idea came to Anne. These men probably came rarely to Almer, and would likely have only a vague idea of what Jane looked like. She smoothed out her clothes and raced down the servants' stairs, three steps at a time, almost tripping but saving herself by grabbing the wooden balustrade. At the ground floor, she found herself next to a service door that led out to the courtyard, and she went through this, adjusting her pace to the slow step appropriate for the person in charge.

"Good morrow, Mistress Tichborne," said the short man as she approached.

Anne had now grown to almost the same height as Jane, and her thick riding-kirtle helped hide her youthful figure. Thinking back to the times she had pretended to be a boy, she thought: 'Disguise isn't really about how you look – it's about how you act.' "Good morrow," she said, trying to copy the tone of command that her mother used when organising the household, though her hands were cold at the thought of how awful it would be if her sister appeared.

"Thank you for bringing these goods over from Lydlinch."

"Our pleasure, good mistress. We was told to put them in the shed with the green door, I trust that is correct?"

"Our plans have changed, my husband asked that they be put straight into these two wagons." Anne indicated the carts that she guessed were destined for Athelhampton. "They are almost full, but if you lift the covers I'm sure you will find some space."

"'Twill be done, Mistress Tichborne."

The short man picked up a heavy sack from the Brune cart and heaved onto his shoulder, followed by the tall man, who grumbled as he carried another

sack that had a small, worn leather pouch attached to it, reminiscent of one used by Robert for small tools. Anne turned away and hurried through the house towards the main entrance. As she went, a thought came to her mind and she felt herself squirming as she thought, 'I did this to help Jane, and Chidiock, but even so, 'tis bad to have done it behind her back.'

At the front door, Jane was laughing as she said, "And what did you think of the privy?"

The mention of the privy reminded Anne that she hadn't had a chance to use it, and she put her worries about impersonation out of her mind and joined in her sister's laughter. "'Twas a most wonderful modern convenience, and I will look forward to using it again before I go home!"

Chapter 10

Cumberground

Anne turned her head at the sound of rumbling, seeing two carts drawn by straining carthorses turning slowly into Athelhampton's rear courtyard, and completely missing the ball that Jane had thrown. It thumped onto the grass beside her bare feet and Little Elizabeth raced over to swap places, crying out: "Cumberground, Aunt Anne, you're a Cumberground! You must go in the middle now!"

"That's not a word to be used by a young lady!" Anne laughed, adding, "Or so the adults say – I don't think it's really too bad!"

Lizzie appeared from the back of the house, waving urgently, and Anne started to pull on her shoes.

"You're not stopping just because you have to go in the middle, are you?" asked Jane.

"No, of course not! Lizzie's telling me I've got to help her with something, I'll be back in a few minutes."

In the rear courtyard, Master Bond's men had just undone the traces from the sweating horses and were leading them away from the carts.

"Are you sure these are the right wagons?" whispered Lizzie, who was watching alongside

Robert and a young lad who wore a mason's overall so new that the brass buckles still gleamed.

"Yes, I recognise them from yesterday," said Anne, "and those poor horses look exhausted, which they would be, hauling all that gold."

"But how can we get it out without being seen?" whispered Lizzie as the men started to untie the covers.

"Master Bond himself isn't here," Anne replied softly, "so perhaps I can make an excuse." She turned to the men and said, "There are a few items of mine on these carts, I need to make sure they don't get muddled up with Jane's things."

"Very good, Mistress Anne," said one of the men. "If you just show us, we'll get them out for you."

"That's kind, but there's no need, Robert and his new apprentice will help me."

Anne pointed at the sacks, and the two masons lifted one each, gasping at the weight, carrying them slowly through the door that led from the courtyard into the cellar. Anne found the leather pouch and hid it in the laundry-bag, and then tried to pick up a sack but couldn't move it. "I'll help," said Lizzie, and the two girls together managed to lift it.

"Where are we taking them?" asked Anne, as they slowly carried the weighty bag into the murk of the cellar. "We can't just leave them here, and they're too heavy to lift through the trapdoor into the secret room."

"Robert has a plan," said Lizzie, "I'm not sure what it is."

Anne went back out to the rear yard, and stopped

abruptly, her breath starting to race. Master Bond had appeared and was standing beside the wagons, saying to the men, "Everything on this cart is to go to Mistress Jane's room. And the items on that other one go to the storeroom."

"There's a sack here belonging to Mistress Anne," said one of the men.

Anne's breath was coming in great gulps as she saw that one of the sacks of gold still remained, but she pulled herself up straight and went over to the carts. "Yes, that's mine," she said, "I put it on the cart when I was at Almer yesterday."

Master Bond gave a quizzical look, making Anne feel queasy, but she managed to say, firmly, "I didn't want to weigh Bayard down. Now, Robert, would you help me with it?"

Robert came over and slowly lifted it, and she followed him into the cellar.

The heavy sacks had been piled up under the trapdoor, which was now open, with Lizzie standing guard on them. As Robert added the last one to the pile, there was a creaking sound above, and two ropes descended. "'Tis a pulley." he said, "'Tis strong enough for stone, I reckon 'tis good enough for gold."

"We'll put the gold at the back of the secret room," said Lizzie. "Only Gyb goes in there, so no-one will know!"

Robert tied a bowline knot around the topmost sack with one of the ropes, and gripped the other in both his hands. "Help me," he said, and Anne and Lizzie stood either side of him and they all heaved. Slowly, the bag of gold rose up and through the trapdoor, where the apprentice's hand appeared and swung it out of sight, before sending the empty rope back down for the next load.

By the time all the gold had been safely stashed in the secret cupboard, Anne's hands were sore. Lizzie looked at them and said, "There is some salve from Friar Wytterage in the back parlour. Come, I will put it on thy fingers."

Anne rubbed her hands firmly together to make sure all the ointment had soaked in, and said, "Let's go up to my room now, and see what's in that leather bag!"

They sat down on Anne's bed, and Lizzie took the pouch out from her laundry-bag. A thick leather strap was sewn into the flap that closed it, its other end held to the rest of the bag by a metal clasp with a small keyhole in it.

"We don't have the key!" said Lizzie.

"No, but we can unstitch the strap. Pass me my sewing-bag, I will find the best needle."

Anne unpicked stitches until there were only a few left. She gave a sharp pull, they all came out at once, and the bag swung open. She put her hand in and drew out some rolled-up documents.

As she unwound the first, a chill spread across her chest. "It's a bill of sale, from William Hunt and Sons, London, for three matchlock breech-loading guns, to be delivered to Chidiock Tichborne."

"Guns!" said Lizzie. "What does he want weapons for?"

Anne put her finger to her lips, and whispered, "When I was at Almer yesterday, Jane said that Chidiock is involved in something very dangerous.

He wants Mary to seize the throne, and bring back the old religion!"

"Mary in place of our dear Queen Elizabeth? That's terrible!" Lizzie whispered back.

"And there would be a fight – that must be why they want guns."

"But many people would die in the battle, it might involve whole armies. The old wars between different kings went on for years and years. And this would be about religion, people fight hardest of all over that."

Anne nodded, as she looked at the other documents. "Here's another bill of sale, it's for more weapons: a dozen swords. The next one is for daggers. And there's one more, it's for chartering a ship. He's foolish to have his name on these – but Jane says he's become obsessed, so I suppose he doesn't care about the risks."

"Thank goodness we've hidden the gold. That will stop them – they needed the weapons, but now they have no way to pay for them!"

Anne frowned silently and took a deep breath before saying, "When I foiled their plan with the ships, they didn't get the new supporters they'd hoped for. But even so, they moved on to the next stage of their plot, thinking they could use Henry's gold to get all these weapons. Now we've stopped that, but I think…" She stopped, hesitant to follow her thoughts to their logical conclusion.

"You think they'll find some other way to continue their plot?"

"I think Chidiock will. He just doesn't seem able to give up. Jane told me about all the meetings he has with people who want to put Mary on the throne."

"At least we've got a bit of time – without the gold, it will take him a while to plan what to do. But he's in London. How can we find out about it, and stop him?"

"I'm going to tell Jane everything we've found out. I'll suggest she goes to stay with him. She's the best person to try and persuade him to stop."

Anne bent her head down and put her hands across her eyes, and Lizzie watched her silently for a minute, before saying softly, "And what about Henry?"

Anne raised her head again and looked at her friend. "He told Eliza that all he would ever do was to provide gold – and he doesn't have any left. So he can't do anything more."

"But someone might still find out that he's been involved!"

"I know. And that made me think about the last line of the poem: '*set the blameless free*'."

"But he's not *blameless*!"

"Money can be given for lots of reasons. You and I know that he gave the gold for a bad purpose, but maybe other people can be persuaded that he did it innocently. Remember that Chidiock had two parchments at Harvest Supper? One held the poem, so perhaps the other gives some kind of evidence that can help Henry – make him look *blameless*."

"And the clues in the poem will show us where to find that second parchment! Let's look at our map and try to see where it points to!"

Anne took the map and her writing materials out from her chest, saying, "We did the ones about the *babes* and the *mansion* right at the beginning, and since then we've solved *Symonds* and the *monk*, and I marked those as well."

"That just leaves the ones about the *bells* and the *door* – do you have any ideas on those?"

"Yes, I had one, but I'm not sure about it."

"Say it anyway!"

Anne hesitated. Worried at seeming silly in front of Lizzie, she looked down at the floor as she said: "*Where waves wash an ancient door.* Could that mean the Durdle Door? The shepherd at Tyneham showed me the path to it along the coast."

Lizzie clapped her hands. "Of course! Everyone in Dorsetshire knows it. That must be it, we should have thought of that before."

Anne let out a deep breath, and smiled. "I'll mark that on the map. That just leaves the *bells*, but I can't think what that means."

"Me neither. But I'll ask Robert. *Symonds* was the only one he recognised first time, but maybe he's thought some more about it. And meanwhile, let's get rid of these documents about the weapons, lest someone find them and use them to arrest Chidiock. Give them to me, and I'll burn them."

Lizzie put her hand on the scrolls, but Anne snatched them away. "No! Don't touch them. I'm sorry to be rude, but I can't let you do that. You could be arrested if anyone found out that you'd destroyed evidence of a treasonous plot."

"But so could you! I want to help!"

"No, it's something I've got to do by myself. You must go now," said Anne, and she squeezed Lizzie's hand and pushed her gently towards the door, and watched as the maid went reluctantly away to her work.

She went over to her small fireplace, where the logs laid early that morning had almost gone out, and fanned them until they began to flame. Her heart beat faster and faster, silently praying that Jane would be able to dissuade Chidiock from further madness, as she fed the documents into the fire one by one, using the poker on each to check that they were completely burnt.

Chapter 11

Unexpected News at the Party

Anne put down the pot of her mother's rose paste that she'd been applying to her cheeks, an ache in the bottom of her stomach as she heard the distinctive sound of hooves from a horse with a slight limp – Jane's beloved piebald. Why come back from London barely a week after setting off? Had Chidiock been quickly persuaded to abandon his plotting, or was there some other reason for such an early return?

She turned to go out to the courtyard, lifting above her ankles the kirtle of wonderful crimson pirate silk that she was wearing for Lizzie and Robert's betrothal party. She caught sight of her face reflected in the window-pane, borrowed charcoal giving an unfamiliar emphasis to her eyebrows, and squirmed – what right had she to be dressing up, when Jane faced who knew what problems?

In the courtyard, a group of adults clustered by the great oaken front door. Their heads were bent low and they spoke in anxious tones. Jane and a liveried servant that Anne didn't recognise wore mud-stained riding gear and the grooms were leading away horses covered in sweat – clearly they had been ridden post-haste from London over the last couple of days. Her parents and Eliza stood alongside, dressed in their fine party clothes.

As Anne approached, Jane was speaking, her voice low and grave, her face damp. "Over the last fortnight, there were many stories circulating round London about a plot against our good Queen. There is nothing so unusual in that, we hear a new one every month or two, but this one seemed especially serious. Worse still, our former priest, Father Ballard, and Babington, the man that Chidiock had been seeing, were said to be involved."

Anne could not restrain herself from crying out, "But you were there with him! Surely he ceased seeing Ballard and Babington when you told him to stop!"

"Of course," said Jane, breaking into open sobs, "I pleaded and pleaded with him. At first, he kept assuring me that all was well, that he was not involved in any plot, and had just spent a few nights with them, drinking and singing as young men do. Then as the rumours became stronger, he admitted they had been making what he called 'plans for a wonderful future,' and that his conscience would not let him stop! And then..." Anne felt great tears rolling down her own face as she leant forward to hear her sister's voice, which had dropped almost to a whisper, "...three nights ago, as we were about to change for bed, there came a thumping on the door, two men burst in, and outside I saw a group of soldiers with halyards... Chidiock crossed himself and kissed me, and I tried to hold him, but they seized him and I cried out to him as they dragged him through the door. I asked where they were going, and they said they were taking him to the Tower, where he would meet his brother Henry."

Jane's voice trailed to nothing and she seemed to stumble into the arms of the Lady Margaret, while Sir Nicholas embraced the weeping Eliza. Anne, struggling to see through her tears, threw her arms around Jane, and then around Eliza, whispering, "Both Chidiock and Henry in the Tower, I can scarce believe it!"

Jane lifted her face and as she began to speak again, her voice barely audible, Anne saw the dark smudges of weeping streaked through the dirt of the journey on her face. "There is more. Next morning, just as I was was leaving to come here, I heard a new rumour. People were saying that the priest Ballard had been set to the torture and made terrible claims: that Babington wrote to Mary, offering to release her through force of arms and... and to murder our good Queen, with the help of six men...Chidiock is identified as one of those men."

Anne had known for so long that disaster lay ahead, but now this went beyond the edges of every nightmare. Thinking of the burnt embers in the fireplace, she cried out: "But what evidence do they have?"

"It seems his link with Babington and Ballard is enough. The only glimmer of hope is that Henry is not one of the six, though they say he is being questioned...no-one knows where that may lead."

Anne's heart seemed to be pounding harder than when she'd lost balance above the swirling waters of the weir near Milton, as she asked quietly: "What will happen to Chidiock?"

Jane said nothing, and after a moment, Sir Nicholas spoke, his voice like a slow growl. "The penalty for treason is to be hung, drawn and quartered."

Jane's face seemed to go grey as she spoke. "There was a moment of hope, of sorts, when we stopped at Putney to water. We heard a new rumour: the Queen did not wish to bc seen glorifying pain, and had issued an edict for humane death, to spare the plotters from the terrible torments..." Her voice trailed off into silence.

Anne let out a long breath. "That, at least, is some small comfort."

"No!" cried Jane. "They say that words from the Queen's courtiers can mean many things, and when we reached Kingston, hard by the royal palace at Hampton Court, we heard a different story – the one that I believe. The Queen issued this command, but told her ministers to make sure that it does not reach the executioners till the second day, when 'twill benefit only the lesser of the plotters. It will come too late to help Chidiock, who is to suffer the full horrors when he is executed on the first day, alongside Babington and his closest fellows."

Anne felt an unfamiliar taste on her lips and realised that the charcoal on her eyebrows had mingled with her tears, and was reminded of what this day had been meant to be. Jane and Eliza were being comforted by her parents and would not miss her for the few minutes it would take to talk with Lizzie and Robert. She slipped away, through the porch and into the Great Hall where masons and farmers, maidservants and milkmaids, all in their best clothes, were standing in small groups mumbling softly, their shoulders slouching. The beer barrels stood unopened and up on the Minstrels' Gallery the musicians were quietly packing their instruments away.

She saw Lizzie and Robert standing by themselves near the fire, raced up to them and hugged them, saying, "I'm so sorry that your party has been ruined."

Robert said, "'Tis of no matter, when poor Chidiock and Henry are in the Tower. Lizzie and I have one another – and 'tis wonderful that you have spared time from your family to come to us."

All three were silent for a minute, until Lizzie said, "If only we could find that second parchment, to help Henry!"

"We need to solve the final clue," said Anne.

"The one about *the bells may ring no more*?" said Robert. "I've been thinking about that. Could it mean one of the fallen-down churches in the deserted villages that I've been collecting stones from?"

"Yes," said Anne, "but you said there were several, so how do we know which one?"

"That's easy," said Robert, "there's one called Ringstead, on the coast. So I think that's the one. It's a play on words."

Here was the solution to the final clue, and on another day, Anne would have been jumping with excitement. But now, she just nodded and said softly, "Well done."

"But what's the next step?" said Lizzie. "We can't just go and search for a parchment in a ruined church or castle, or at Durdle Door, or even here at

Athelhampton. It could be almost anywhere in those places."

"There must be some way to interpret the solutions that we've found," said Robert. "We should all think about it, one of us will work out the answer sooner or later."

"That might take too long!" cried Lizzie. "Henry might get put on trial long before we work it out."

"But there is something I can do," said Anne. "I'm going to ride to dark old Wardour castle tomorrow and tell William that the second parchment exists, even though we haven't found it yet. He seems to be connected with the government, maybe he can do something!"

"He might be suspicious of you," said Lizzie.

Robert nodded. "He thinks too much: such men are dangerous."

Anne felt her hands go clammy as she said, "There are risks. But one of the reasons why Chidiock gave me the poem was because I knew William. So, I have to go."

Chidic

North-East
The Symonds
Castle falls

North-West
The bells may
• ring no more

The sea-

Where waves wash
an ancient door

's Poem

- Where thee as babe and
  babes of thine confine

r Frome

South-East
A lord now wears
the monkish robes

South-West
A family mansion
Looking out to sea

Chapter 12
Old Wardour Castle

Anne could smell the dankness of the old walls of the Arundells' castle, and feel their cold chilling her toes even through the thickness of her riding-boots. She pressed her legs against the familiar warmth of Bayard's flanks and glanced gratefully at Sir George's friendly, military frame beside her. The great dark tower, the tallest she'd ever seen, rose ahead of them, dominating the landscape visible for miles across Cannock Chase, which she knew was once a hunting-ground of old King Henry.

"I'm glad ye have come with me," she said.

Her uncle laughed. "'Tis my pleasure. And anyway, I'm following orders – thy mother told me I must come with ye as chaperone, as soon as she heard ye was set on coming here."

"Chaperone? I'm not here to see a suitor!"

"Guardsman, then. 'Tis better to have two rather than one in this damp ancient tower, where bodies can disappear too easily into deep dungeons. But have no worry that I will interfere, ye is commander of this expedition and I will keep as silent as I can."

They rode into the outer courtyard and dismounted, handing the reins to waiting ostlers, and Anne followed the old soldier towards the great entrance steps. She shivered as she looked up at the

Arundell arms, six martlets with fussy tails, thinking how different this visit was from her previous one last Yuletide. Then, she and her sisters had bantered happily over whether the simple little birds in the windows at Athelhampton were better.

As the servants opened the tall wooden doors she glanced back towards the stables to check that Bayard was being treated well. Beside one of the ostlers, she saw an unpleasantly familiar face in an utterly unexpected livery. It was Walter Bearde, wearing a black coat emblazoned with six silver martlets – the Arundell livery. In surprise and fear, her foot slipped on the steps, and she had to grab Sir George's arm to stop herself falling.

An hour later, clutching her elegant blue silk kirtle tight around her for warmth, Anne followed a servant through one murky corridor after another, the bulky figure of Sir George beside her as they passed successive side passages sloping downwards into damp-smelling darkness. Finally a door was opened and she had to shield her eyes from the light of a hundred candles, as they were ushered into a great room heated by two glowing fires.

Clearly this was where William received guests, but the birds on the servant's livery kept reminding her of Walter, and she tensed herself to force her mind back to her host, who she must be ready to greet when he appeared. The walls were covered from floor to ceiling in fine tapestries, depicting noble knights spearing wolves and rescuing maidens from tall crags, and she watched the servant draw one of them aside to reveal a doorway through which William strode, resplendent in crimson silk under his dark hair.

"My Lord Arundell," the servant declaimed, and Anne steadied her breath, thinking: 'This is far finer garb than he wore at Athelhampton, these clothes reveal his true identity as a powerful servant of royalty. But this is still the diffident younger son who talked to me by the dovecote and shied away from courtship – I must not be intimidated by him.'

William bowed to them. "Sir George, Mistress Anne, most welcome." Anne curtseyed as her uncle bowed, and their host walked to a chair to the left of the bigger fire and motioned them to the right. The engraving on the silver goblet beside her matched the pattern on Walter's livery, and without pausing to think about politeness, she put her hand out and turned it to hide this new reminder of him.

"'Tis the finest Madeira," said William, "a favourite of mine," and as Anne took a sip she had to swallow hard to avoid retching, for it was stronger than anything she had tasted. He continued, "I trust you had a good journey?"

"Thank you, my Lord," said Sir George, "the ride was a fine one, and we are most grateful that you have received us. My niece is deeply concerned about the misfortunes that have befallen her brothers, and has important information that she wishes to discuss with you."

Anne found William's eyes, which had been locked on her uncle's face, now suddenly fixed on her as he said: "I am so sorry that it has come to this, for your brothers Chidiock and Henry."

Breathing deep as she tried to put the grandness of William's room and apparel out of her mind and remember the shy man beside her in the garden, Anne said, "I am here to speak about Henry, if I may have your leave to do so?"

"Mistress Anne, you are free to speak on whatever matter you wish."

"Do you know why Henry has been arrested?"

Anne noticed a slight pause before William responded: "The matter is, of course, an affair of State, and not one that can be discussed officially. But I respect the concern for a close relative that has brought you here. And so, I can tell you unofficially, that he promised Chidiock gold, to be used to buy arms to further an evil enterprise against our good Queen. Strangely, the gold never arrived, forcing the plotters to abandon their original plans and proceed instead with a new version of their foul scheme, using borrowed weapons – but the mere promise of the gold is enough to implicate Henry."

"I think there has been a misunderstanding." William looked at Anne quizzically as she continued: "Henry did promise gold to Chidiock, but it was help him and my dear sister Jane buy the house at Almer that they've been renting. It's perfect for them to raise a family in, and it's close to Athelhampton."

Anne felt as though the bright light of the candles was fading until all she could see was the darkness of William's eyes. "That," he said, "is a fine yarn, such as might be spun in a tavern of an evening, and coming from the sister of a man under threat of his life in the Tower, few might believe it..."

Anne, unable to stop herself, interrupted. "There is a parchment, which gives evidence."

"A parchment? What kind of evidence?"

"I don't have it, but I'm sure it proves that the gold was to buy the house, though I don't know the exact detail. I'm searching for it, and I'm sure I will find it soon."

"That is hard to believe."

"You trusted me enough before, to ask me to act on your behalf. It was you who were not open, you came as a suitor, yet you wanted me as a spy, a spy on my own family, not as a wife."

"That is unfair. 'Twas your mother, the Lady Margaret, who told you I was a suitor. I never said any word to press my suit. I have not been seeking a wife, not at Athelhampton nor anywhere else, and nor will I in future."

He stood up abruptly and said, "I will make one small promise. I will use such influence as I have to delay the sentencing of your brother Henry for a short while. Maybe that will give you time to find this parchment. And if you do, you should bring it to me, yourself." He looked at her closely. "I will accept it from no-one else."

Anne stood as well, and Sir George spoke as he drew himself up to his full soldierly height. "I thank you for your time, my Lord."

"It was my pleasure. And now I trust that you will enjoy your evening, I believe the cook is preparing one of his special pies, which he always does uncommonly well."

"'Tis one of those mysteries," said William, smiling across the table at Anne, "that squab pie is called that, when it contains mutton, and not squab."

Anne smiled, glad that her host was back to being his charming self, now that the serious discussions were behind them. She said, "What's in a name? Your cook does an excellent job, 'tis the best I have tasted." She drew tight the shawl that she wore over her thick winter kirtle and three layers of smocks, thinking that Wardour was the coldest place she had ever stayed in, and that the pie was the only thing better than at Athelhampton.

The servers had cleared the table, and the candles

were starting to gutter. "And now, 'tis time to retire," said William. "In the morning I must leave early, to ride to a kinsman at Sutton Place."

"That is a long journey, well beyond Winchester," said Sir George. "but ye will be rewarded for the ride, for I hear there is good hunting there."

"Alas, I will have no time to enjoy it, for I ride onwards to London on the after-morrow, where I stay for a week on business."

With Sir George on one side and William on the other, Anne set off towards the staircase that led up to their bedrooms, passing the tables that stretched the length of Wardour's Great Hall. All along the benches sat guests in the leather doublets of merchants or the smocks of farmers, alongside the officers of the house in their Arundell livery, but she saw no-one familiar, until her eye was drawn to a head of close-cropped white hair. She said, "Good Master Blanke, well met."

The Moor stood up and bowed. "Well met indeed, young Mistress Anne. Only this evening did I find out thy name – my apologies not to have known when ye came to my stall." Anne felt a slight tremor in her hands; was it coincidence that both Walter and the Moor, who had been in Dorchester market on the day she had burned the pitch, were at Wardour on the same day that she was? He continued, "I am here to offer fine jewellery to the ladies of the house, and would be most happy to show a selection to you, since I hear ye have now recovered the pearls you mentioned when we last met?"

The tremor worsened, as Anne wondered whether it was Walter who had told the Moor about Young John returning the pearls to her, and if so, why had he? But she replied politely, "You are most kind, and perhaps on another occasion."

They approached the stairs, Anne pulling her clothes tighter around her as she looked at the cold stone steps winding upwards, but before they reached them an ostler approached Sir George and said, "My Lord, might I ask you 'bout feed for your horses?"

Anne felt another tremor, stronger than before, for she recognised the speaker as the man who had been standing beside Walter under the arch when they had arrived that morning. He was now joined by four other men, who surrounded Sir George and separated him from her.

A voice came at her elbow, and as she turned she felt a cold far deeper than any from the stones, for there was Walter himself, the black of his Arundell livery a stark contrast to the crimson scar down his cheek.

"My Lord," he said, in his low rasping voice, "I have discovered that Mistress Anne, far from being an innocent sister, has been most closely involved in plotting with her brothers Henry and Chidiock."

Anne felt the half-digested squab pie starting to rise up through her gullet, but she managed to cry out, "That is outrageous! I have done nothing!"

"This is a most serious allegation," said William, his dark eyes staring hard at Anne before moving to Walter. "Pray tell us of the evidence." As he spoke, Anne heard movement behind and glancing back, saw that two bulky men in William's livery were now blocking her way back to the Great Hall.

"I saw her," said Walter, "in Dorchester market, with the vendors of pitch, which was to be used to burn the town in a most foul raid by French ships, organised by Henry's kinsman. Clearly she was part of the plot. Then just a month ago, Henry had some documents in a pouch, no doubt for some sinister purpose, and a carter told me she ordered it placed on a wagon, intending to hide or destroy it!"

Anne squeezed her fists in outrage at the first accusation, trying to put the second out of her mind. "'Tis the opposite! In Dorchester, I wasn't helping the plot. I spoke to the merchants to find out what was happening, so I could stop it." She looked straight into William's eye. "This man Walter used to work for someone who has a feud against me, I think he may have taken service with you so that he can spread falsehoods about me, as his former master did." As she spoke, she saw that Sir George was now surrounded by five men, and she thought: 'He has been in many battles, but even he cannot succeed against so many opponents.'

William said to Walter, "A grudge may colour a man's view – are there other witnesses?"

"Yes, there was a stallholder, the good Moor here, who saw her with the sellers of pitch."

The jeweller, standing near, nodded his head slowly.

Anne's chest was burning as she said, "Standing near to a merchant selling pitch is no crime, and I bought nothing. But what I did do, was to throw the torches and destroy those evil plans utterly!"

William looked deeply into her eyes. "'Twill do your cause no good to make absurd claims. 'Tis well known, many people were watching: that was no girl, it was some young village lad, out for a dare."

Anne found herself imagining the dank smells of a filthy cell in the Tower and the sound of an executioner sharpening his blade. She could feel Walter's triumphant gaze on her, hear the murmur of unpleasant talk among his companions.

She looked away from all these hostile figures at the only friendly person there, and she was reminded of the gift he had given her, the brown of its flanks contrasting with a single white streak, and she knew what she had to say.

"The birthmark!" Her cry rang out loud and she could hear it echo back from the roof above. "Bayard's birthmark! The cloth that was covering it fell off, Walter must have seen it when I threw the torches."

There was a sudden silence all around, as William gazed at Anne, then turned slowly to Walter and said, "Is it true? Did you see it?"

Anne felt nauseous as she looked at Walter, who stood sullenly. How would he reply to this direct question from his master? He gave an unpleasant laugh, shrugged his shoulders and said, "I wasn't looking that way, I could not say."

Anne squeezed her hands together in anger at this falsehood – she knew he had been looking straight at her. But then another voice came.

"I saw the birthmark. A vivid white against the brown everywhere else." It was Blanke. "I saw no reason to mention it before, for I have never seen the young mistress' horse and did not know it was hers."

There was silence across the Great Hall. The servants had stopped moving plates, the guests' conversation had stopped. After a moment, William spoke again, his voice low and serious as he looked at Walter, saying, "Mistress Anne acted innocently in Dorchester, indeed she was most helpful to the Crown. As for thy other accusation, do ye have any evidence, beyond the carter's hearsay?"

"Nay," said Walter, his voice more hesitant than before, "but I do not trust her at all!"

"Bearde, I abide by evidence, not personal vendettas. If ye believe that Mistress Anne is acting against the Crown, come to me with proof that none can dispute."

The pain in Anne's chest subsided as the men who had been clustering around her and Sir George stepped back.

William said, "I thank you, Mistress Anne, for thy actions at Dorchester, but I must warn you as well. With Chidiock and Henry in the Tower, accused of the worst crime imaginable, my instructions to Bearde and his men remain. They will watch you – anything you do to support the plotters would be evidence against you. Young as you are, the full force of the law applies." He bowed, and continued in a softer tone, "So take the greatest care, for I would not wish anything bad to befall you. I wish you a safe journey home." Anne curtseyed to William and with the eyes of Walter and his men staring at her, she gripped Sir George's arm tightly, and hurried away to the far end of the hall where the staircase led up to their bedrooms.

She went through a heavy curtain into a lobby at the foot of the steps, and found the Moor waiting there. She said, "I thank ye, good Master Blanke, for thy words."

The old man bowed, and spoke quietly. "When my father was a young man, the Martyns did him a great service, so I was glad to be able help ye."

"A great service?"

"My father was a trumpet-player with Queen Catherine, Princess she was then, and stayed in thy house at Athelhampton. No-one in England knew him, but thy ancestor invited him to play in the Great Hall, so he became famous among the English Knights and later worked for old King Henry."

"And do ye also play the trumpet?"

The stallholder laughed. "I had not the talent to learn music, but my father taught me many other things, and most important was that a favour is never forgotten."

Through a gap in the curtains that separated their lobby from the dining hall, Anne caught Walter's eyes; he was barely a dozen paces away. Blanke followed her gaze, and lowered his voice almost to a whisper, so only she could hear. "Truth be told, 'twas difficult to see thy horse through the smoke. But tonight, when I realised that a Martyn was in danger, suddenly my memory of it became as clear as on a Spring morning!"

Anne could still feel Walter's eyes on hers, and anxious lest he learn this secret, said nothing. Instead she smiled and bowed her thanks to the Moor, before putting her arm firmly through Sir George's and turning to the steps. As they went upstairs, the old soldier said, "I will keep watch outside the door of thy room tonight and we will leave at dawn. I trust no-one in this dank old castle."

Chapter 13
A Most Notable Coward

Next night, back at Athelhampton, Anne went to bed early, exhausted and keen to make up for her very short sleep at Wardour. She found herself dreaming of dark twisted horrors, with cries of rage and pain in the darkness. Gradually she realised that she was half-waking from her nightmare, for there really were sounds of people talking, quietly but with anger and fear in their voices.

She stole out of bed, and slipped through the small door to the Minstrels' Gallery where she crouched, invisible. Gyb lay silently beside her, his green eyes staring intently at the scene below. The Great Hall was lit by only a single candle, which cast a shadow across her father's bearded face even as it lit the sharp, sad beauty of Jane, sitting close beside him at the long table.

Sir Nicholas' voice echoed round the Hall. "Bribery? No! No Martyn man will ever pay gold for such a crime."

"Father, they will cut him, tear him, I cannot think of the pain." It was Jane's voice, imploring, and Anne thought she saw the light catch a tear. "I have heard stories, people give the executioner gold, he makes it look as though the victim is tortured to death, but 'tis a feint!"

Sir Nicholas got up and came to sit on the bench beside Jane, embracing her and now speaking softly. "I know thy love for Chidiock is deep and true. But he is beyond our help now. They are determined to avenge this plot against the Queen – blood will have blood! If the knife does not do its job, all London will know who has paid – and bribery is a dire crime in itself. Ye might be the next one to be arrested."

Jane sobbed out loud and Anne clenched her fists, thinking, 'Fight back, stand your ground, he knows not where his words lead.'

Jane was speaking through her tears. "Father, he is my husband until the last drop of life is taken from him, screaming in front of the crowd. I care nothing for the future, I care not whether I am arrested, nor that the whole world knows that the Martyns paid gold to save one of theirs!"

"I cannot allow ye to take the risk. Ye are too precious to me."

As Anne heard these words, she was reminded of the stories she'd heard from Tom, lawyer husband of her sister Frances, about judges who condemn a man with no hope of appeal. She watched Sir Nicholas stand up, turn his back and walk away to his rooms, leaving Jane alone with that single sad flame.

No need to go down to her, she was coming up and Anne was ready, arms out, embracing her, her own dear, cold, devout Jane, now warm and sobbing. A sister, thought Anne, is here to give solace, but also succour.

"He forbade you, and he said no Martyn man," Anne whispered, "but he forbade nothing of other Martyn women."

"What can you do?" Jane whispered back. "You have no gold, and if you did, you have no means to give it to the man who wields the knife."

Anne squeezed her hand. An image of Endy, reaching up to the ceiling to save her, came into her mind, and she said: "Dear sister, I have both."

Anne looked at the lad who had taken the reins. The moonlight picked out a scar, white against his dirty jacket, that stretched from his throat to his ear. She wondered who might have inflicted such a large wound on someone whose head barely reached the top of Bayard's thigh.

"I'll water and feed him for 'ee, if 'ee pay me well," he said, spitting out his words rudely, "and maybe find 'ee a lighter mount to suit 'ee better." It was a boy's voice, yet as Anne dismounted, she was suddenly reminded of a visit with Christopher to the horse-traders at Dorchester market, who had scanned each animal's height and teeth to calculate its worth, just as this lad seemed to be doing.

"He best be waiting for me, fit and well, when I return," she said sharply, handing him a small coin from the pouch at her waist, "I come for Captain Heynes and Roger Munday, and be warned, I will tell them he is in thy care." Even before she finished, she saw that the mere mention of the pirate and his inn-keeping bosun had changed the lad's cocky stare to lowered eyes and slumping shoulders.

Heaving the heavy saddlebags, one in each hand, she searched for the inn door in the moon-shadows cast by the tall towers of Corfe Castle, at last finding it by stumbling on a step and falling against its rough timbers. They swung open and she came into a blaze of light and noise and heat, breathing in the smell of men's sweat and ale. Tall as she now was, among this press of leather jerkins and pewter and sheathed blades, she was reminded of those days when, much smaller, no-one had ever taken any notice of her.

Past gold-ringed earlobes and trying to hold her breath against the stink of stale urine, Anne reached the narrow wooden bar across a door at the back. Behind it stood a middle-aged woman, whose muscular arms were tattooed with men on gibbets and who said, "What want ye? There is no place for young women in my house."

Anne took a deep breath, the smell of ale welcome against the background whiff of vomit. "I'm here for Captain Heynes and bosun Munday," she said.

The woman's brows creased deeper as she stared at Anne. "Bosun Munday? How dare ye! If ye have an assignment with my man, I'll beat him to Kingdom Come and have ye strung up at Studland Beach."

"The good captain and I," Anne strove to avoid more talk of gibbets, "our lives were saved in the same way, it makes us like brother and sister. He promised me help, I need to see him, as soon as I can."

"Brother and sister? This is a good tale to add to the long list that never yet earned the teller a free

beer." The lines above the eyes eased but slightly, as the speaker disappeared into the doorway.

A moment later, there was the Captain, velvet immaculate and lace ruffs white in the candlelight, bowing low.

"Mistress Anne, ye is most welcome, your noble presence shines brighter than ever in this foul hell-hole. Your business must be of the greatest urgency to have risked the road in the dark."

"Well met, good Captain, and 'twas not so dark nor so dangerous, for the moon shines bright and my horse is as sure-footed as any on the road."

"'Tis good to hear. But now, come away, this is no place for ye," and he lifted the counter, beckoning her into a back room.

Dark brown, the drink was so hot it almost burned her mouth, her senses suddenly more alert and her mind more awake than from any ale or wine. Stephen Heynes laughed out loud as he watched her.

"'Tis a potent brew, stronger than any summoned up by that old witch Ma Melemouth! I took it from a Spaniard, who got it from Malta, where the Turkish prisoners drink it. It comes in small brown pods." The gibbeted arm topped up the Captain's tankard from a massive jug. "Anne, meet Mistress Munday, wife of my shipmate the Bosun Munday, and keeper of this fine house. And Mistress Munday, meet Anne, my sister-in-arms, for we both owe our lives to the same small being, God rest him," and here he lifted his pewter for a deep draft and Anne took a more cautious sip of her brown brew, at once both excited and alarmed at the energising effect it was having on her.

"I need you to bribe an executioner for me," said Anne, keen to get down to the matter at hand before the Captain had consumed much more ale. "My brother-in-law, Chidiock Tichborne, must be saved. Jane, my sister, will be at the scaffold to watch, and I have promised her that it will be a mock execution so they can escape together afterwards."

Heynes took a draught from his tankard, and then shook his head slowly as he spoke. "Bribery's dangerous. Why take the risk? The last time one of my crew was due for the hemp at Studland, we brought the hangman into this very room the night before, we tickled him with a knife, so he knew what would happen if our shipmate wasn't alive the next eve. No need for a bribe that day, 'nless you account a good quart of Mistress Munday's finest ale."

Anne did not smile. "Good Captain, I wish 'twas here on the Isle of Purbeck, where your writ runs strong. But, 'tis at Holborn Bar, and all London will be watching."

And now Anne heard only the shouts, the burps and the laughter from the front room, for the Captain's loquacity failed him and his first reply was to look her hard in the eyes. Then he spoke:

"Your friend is in this deep indeed, to go to Holborn. There they take the traitors. Your brother must have offended good Queen Bess far beyond what you or I could ever do. And 'tis not an easy death, they cut them and tear out their insides, before they kill them. There will be soldiers, and right in the heart of London Town."

"I have gold worth enough to turn the head of even the Queen's own butcher," said Anne.

"'Tis a fool's errand," Heynes said. "The man will likely take thy gold but break his promise. And," he paused and looked away from Anne. "'Tis a grave crime, a man who is caught bribing the executioner might find himself on the end of the noose, or worse, on the end of the knife."

"I want you to try," said Anne, but she found herself sinking low into her chair as she saw the Captain shaking his head. She continued very quietly, "When I became Endy's owner, ye promised me, that as he had saved thy life, ye would help me when I needed." But she saw that the Captain was still looking away, and shaking his head.

She rose to her feet quite abruptly, knocking over the remains of the hot brown drink, pulled herself up to full height and said, "Then I will go. My horse is outside. At first light he will take me swiftly. I care not for men who do not honour their promises. I will do this myself."

As she spoke, she was starting to think about the scale of the task. She had no idea how to reach London, nor where to go when she got there, nor how to deal with the dangers. But she squeezed her hands into fists and thought, 'Here is a man who is letting me down, it cannot be that difficult to give some money to someone. I will find a way to do it.'

Heynes said nothing, but the landlady, who, Anne realised, must have been quietly listening, now spoke, her voice harsh and loud. "Ye's a most notable coward, an infinite and endless liar, an hourly promise-breaker, the owner of no one good quality! Would ye forget what Endy did for ye, because ye is scared of a few Justices?"

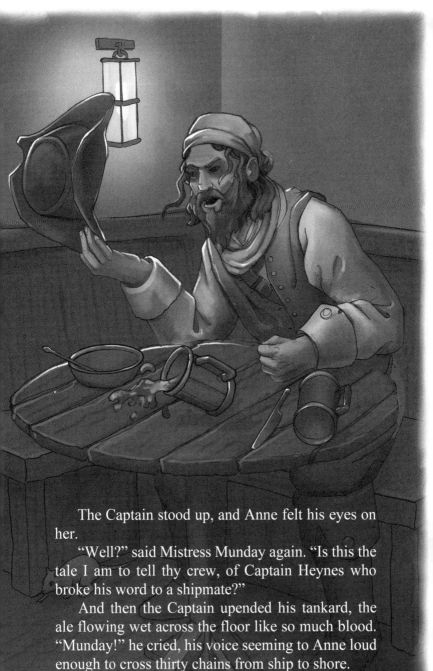

The Captain stood up, and Anne felt his eyes on her.

"Well?" said Mistress Munday again. "Is this the tale I am to tell thy crew, of Captain Heynes who broke his word to a shipmate?"

And then the Captain upended his tankard, the ale flowing wet across the floor like so much blood. "Munday!" he cried, his voice seeming to Anne loud enough to cross thirty chains from ship to shore.

"Clear away this ale! Fetch me the hot brown drink, with bread and beef. Tell that horrible small lad of yours to water and feed my horse. I leave within the hour, and take my chance with the moonlight. When thy worthless husband appears, he is to follow me at once, with three hard fellows."

Anne looked at Heynes, his eyes seeming to blaze brightly, with all sign of drunkenness banished, and she gave a broad smile of gratitude to Mistress Munday, who winked back before turning to look at the Captain. "I will fetch thy victuals, and I will find thy dark coat and hot water for shaving. That Albion tavern at Wimborne, 'tis used by the Queen's messengers, and ye should look the part of a wealthy merchant lest someone there recognises a man back from the dead."

The Captain growled. "I take not that road. Much better, I take a boat from Studland. That will keep me hidden from the prying eyes of the Queen's men without need of the razor. I'll be across the water to Poole by first light, they never go that way."

Mistress Munday nodded and hurried out of the door, and Heynes turned to Anne. "Two day's hard ride, the changes of horse will cost at least three sovereigns for me and my crew. A couple more to persuade the lads in the alehouses of Putney to tell me where that butcher hides himself, and when I find him, I doubt that he'll settle for less than fifty. So I hope thy sacks of gold are full." He took the two heavy bags, weighed them in his hands for a moment, nodded, and strode away.

If the pirate did his task, Anne thought, Chidiock's life would be saved, though he would have to leave England forever. For Henry, there was a chance to both save his skin, and also have him declared innocent and able to go home – but only if she found the parchment. Remembering how William had said that she had very little time to get it to him before sentence was passed, she drew her riding-kirtle round her and made towards the door.

Mistress Munday came back into the room. "Where is ye going, young mistress?"

"I have to hurry home at once, my other brother-in-law needs help!"

"'Tis ye who will need help, if ye stumble into the Frome in the dark. There are clouds about, the moonlight can be a false friend. I have a nice straw mattress for ye upstairs and in the morning ye can do what has to be done with a clear head and good light."

Anne looked at the landlady whose face was smiling but whose large arms were set firm on her hips, and said, "'Tis good counsel, Mistress Munday, I will accept thy kind lodgings with thanks, but please make sure that I am woken at dawn!"

Chapter 14
The Second Parchment

Anne was roused at first light by Mistress Munday and hurried to the stables. The small lad had changed into an almost respectable doublet and was making a passable job of rubbing down Bayard's flanks, earning himself another small coin. Once on the road, she pushed on quickly, until she came near to Wareham, where there was a great crush of slow-moving carts queuing to cross the bridge over the river Frome that gave access to the town.

As she inched forward, stopping and starting, Anne jiggled the reins up and down in her frustration at not reaching home quickly. But there was no way to go faster and she gradually became calm enough to exchange banter with some lads sitting on a pile of stone cartwheels in the wagon in front of her.

"Did ye ride up from Swanage, mistress?" the boldest one cried. "Ye did well to get through Corfe without the pirates stealing that fine horse from ye!"

"Just let them try!" said Anne, laughing.

This talk of riding from the sea at Swanage up to the river Frome at Wareham put the inkling of an idea into her mind, and it began to take shape as the queue moved a little faster and she crossed the bridge. An image of the map came to her; she had drawn the coast and the rivers as horizontal lines, but there were no verticals. If she added a line from the sea at Swanage up to the Frome at Wareham, running from bottom to almost the top of the map on the right hand side, and a similar line to the left, she would have a complete rectangle. She wasn't yet sure what that would mean, but it seemed worth trying.

Once past the market stalls and the fortifications that ringed the ancient town, she was on the open road, but she wanted to let her thoughts develop calmly, so she held Bayard back to a trot. She kept up the same sedate pace through Affpuddle and on to Tolpuddle, ideas still churning in her mind, and as the chimneys of Athelhampton appeared in the distance she gave a gentle sigh of contentment.

She rode into the stables and had barely had time to dismount when Lizzie raced in, holding her skirts above her ankles against the mess on the floor, and calling out, "Did you see Heynes? Will he take the gold to London?"

"Yes," said Anne. "He was reluctant for a while, but the wife of his bosun, who you'd want to have on your side if you were in a fight, reminded him about Endy – then he agreed to do it." As she spoke, she looked out through the door towards the graves in the nearby churchyard, and felt her eyes moisten.

"And there's news here: early this morning, Jane set off back to London."

Anne dried her face on her sleeve and looked again at Lizzie. "That's good to hear. She can arrange a safe place for Chidiock to go, after the mock execution, and find a ship that will take him to France."

"And I've been thinking about the map. My geography is not so good, but I've realised that the compass-points make no sense. The *family mansion looking out to sea* is to the south-east of the other places, not the south-west as it says in the poem. The *Symonds castle* is north-east in the poem, but on the map, it's in the north-west. The others are wrong as well!"

Anne was nodding as she listened. "You're right, I hadn't thought of that, but I see it now. And it starts to fit with the idea I had while I was riding home."

Lizzie looked over to the sundial, just visible above the gate into the courtyard. "I wish there was time to talk more, but I need to go," she said. "I've got to work on the evening meal, my father was furious last time I was late. He says it's not fair on the others, they think it's because I'm his daughter – and because you're my friend."

Anne blushed, and she called out as Lizzie dashed away, "I'm sorry, and I won't hold you up in future!"

Up in her room, Anne changed out of her riding clothes, opened the chest and pulled out the map and quill. She laid the parchment out and drew a more or less vertical line from the sea-coast up to the Frome river on the right, roughly along the route that the lads thought she had ridden that morning. She drew a matching one on the left of the map. She held it up and looked at it: a rectangle, with slightly wavy edges.

Chidioc

North-East
The Symonds
Castle falls

North-West
The bells may
ring no more

The sea

Where waves wa
an ancient doo

Poem

- Where thee as babe and
  babes of thine confine

Frome

South-East
A lord now wears
the monkish robes

South-West
A family mansion
Looking out to sea

She stared and stared at the map, trying to pull her thoughts together, and decided that the only way to make that happen was to discuss them with someone else. She pulled on her shoes, pushed the map into her pocket and hurried down to the Great Hall, hoping to find Lizzie serving the midday meal. But she'd spent too long poring over the map – the tables were empty, with menservants clearing away the last remains of food.

She raced across the back courtyard towards the kitchen, calling out "Lizzie! Where are you?" A delicious smell of fresh baking came from the open door of the kitchen and as she came in, she saw that a batch of patties was being taken out of the new baking-oven on the far wall.

"Master Moryshe," she cried. "Where's Lizzie? I need to find her quickly! And … please may I have one of those patties?"

"Lizzie is just in the laundry," said the head cook. "But, Mistress Anne, please don't interrupt her from her work, 'tis not fair on her fellows."

Anne looked down at the ground and said, "I'm sorry, Master Moryshe, you're right, of course, I won't stop her working, but is it alright if I help her and talk while we work together?"

The head cook laughed. "'Tis a good solution! And as for the patties, they are for the evening, but I heard ye were not in Hall for the midday meal, so ye may have one – but only one!"

Anne thanked him, picked up the patty as she ran out into the yard, stuffing half of it into her mouth as she went and almost bumping into Lizzie, who was coming out of the laundry, a wicker basket full of neatly-folded linens on her arm.

Anne swallowed hurriedly and said, "Is there another basket that I can carry?"

"Why, yes, there is one by the door."

As Anne picked up the heavy laundry, she said, "I have a new idea about solving the poem!"

"Tell me quickly, while we carry this through to the Great Hall."

"We should go to the Marriage Chamber, and look there!"

"Why there? I can't take time off, my father's being much stricter."

"But we must!"

"Maybe I can find a way. Eliza let her children play there yesterday, before they went home. It needs a good dust, and I'm sure there'll be toys left behind. I'll see whether I can be allowed to clear them up and clean in there as my next task!"

"And I'll help you!"

They delivered the linen, and Lizzie went off to get permission while Anne went to get a broom from the parlour.

Up in the Marriage Chamber, Anne took out the map and laid it on the bed so they could look at it as they worked, and she started dusting in a corner just as Lizzie came in. As they arranged wooden blocks and other lost toys in a neat pile, Anne said, "I think the clue about *babes* may hold the key."

"That was the easiest one of all, Little Elizabeth solved it straight away! Athelhampton is where you were born, and where you will have your own babies."

"I...I don't think those words refer to the whole

of Athelhampton, I think they refer to this room itself! That's my new idea!"

"Are you sure? What made you think of that?"

"I'm not sure, but I think it's worth trying. I got the idea when I was going into Wareham. I realised that if you added lines connecting the coast to the river Frome, it becomes a kind of rectangle – and that made me think of a room! So it isn't a geographic map at all – it's a plan of a room!"

"You think the room is here – because this is where you, and all your sisters, and brothers, God bless their souls, were born?"

"Yes! And this is where I'll be confined when I have my own babies!"

Lizzie's face widened into a big smile. "So, the poem is telling us where to look right here, in this room?"

"Yes!" Anne was smiling as well. "Chidiock and Jane were staying in this room when he wrote the poem. He'd have watched the sun move round, and that would have inspired him to the points of the compass."

"It's late afternoon now, so the sun's coming from the south-west, over there." Lizzie was pointing to the side of the window where the light was flooding in.

"So that corner of the room is *a family mansion looking out to sea*".

"And over to the other side of the window is south-east," cried Lizzie, "so that's where *a Lord now wears the Monkish robes.*"

Anne found herself breathing faster and faster. "Over there is north-east, so that's the Symonds castle, and behind is where *the bells may ring no more*. So the sea-coast is represented by this wall over here."

"The whole point of the riddle was that it leads to *where waves wash an ancient door* – the Durdle Door, which lies on the sea-coast in between Tyneham and the deserted village of Ringstead. So the poem is telling us to search about halfway along this wall!"

Anne ran her hands along the wooden panelling, finding nothing. There was no fireplace on this side of the room where she might find a hidden string, as she'd done when she had once searched for another secret. She tried pushing one of the panels, and nothing happened. Same for the next panel, so she tried pushing much harder, putting her whole weight on the wood. Nothing. She frowned – was her idea wrong, after all? She pressed on the next panel, and again nothing happened.

"You've got to keep trying!" said Lizzie.

Anne pushed the next panel, and it clicked open easily. She almost fell inwards, gasping.

"It's a hidden cupboard! Too shallow for anyone to get into!"

"What's in there?"

"Just some shelves… its murky, I can't see anything." At Anne's feet a black shape appeared from nowhere, and Gyb slipped inside, sniffing along the edges of the floor of the secret space. "Ah! There's something on the bottom shelf…a bag of soft velvet." Anne lifted it out, grinning, and skipped over to the window where there was still some of the late afternoon light. "It's got a drawstring...and look, here's a parchment! It's the larger of the two that Chidiock had at Harvest Supper."

"And tied with the same pretty ribbon as he used for the poem!"

"We've solved the puzzle!" Anne took Lizzie's hands and kissed her on both cheeks.

"You're so clever to think of this room!" said the maid, returning the kisses.

The sun had disappeared and the light was starting to fade. Anne found a candle and lit it before untying the ribbon, unwinding the parchment and starting to read.

"'*A Deed, for the purchase of the Manor at Almer, in Dorsetshire, sold by Christopher Anketill, Guardian of Brownsea Island for Sir Christopher Hutton, to Chidiock Tichborne, the payment by Henry Brune of Lydlinch, Dorsetshire... Dated 15th February, 1586... signed and witnessed, Henry Brune, Christopher Anketill and Chidiock Tichborne.*'"

Anne's shoulders drooped slightly. Lizzie looked at her and said, "You seem disappointed! Do you think it won't be enough to get Henry out of the Tower?"

"I'm not sure," said Anne, slowly. "I remember my father saying that when you buy a house, you go through various stages – and this is only one document. So, it might not be enough evidence in a proper trial. But when I told William about this, he said I must give it to him, in person. Maybe what he meant was that it would be good enough for him."

"But does he have the authority to let Henry go?"

asked Lizzie.

"He...he seems to be quite powerful." Anne lowered her voice. "Powerful enough to almost arrest me!"

"So, ride over to Wardour again, and give it to him! But will he be there?"

"He only went to London a few days ago – so I don't think he'll be back tomorrow. But he could be back any day after that." Anne's hands went clammy as she added, "So, to get the parchment to him as quickly as possible, I'll go there on the after-morrow and stay till he returns – even though it may mean waiting in that grim castle."

ANNE OF ATHELHAMPTON

Chapter 15

The Letter from Captain Heynes

Bayard, his birthmark bright in the afternoon sunlight, neighed gently as Anne came into the stables. She laughed as she saw Gyb sunning himself in the middle of the floor, clearly enjoying Urian's absence on a hunting trip with her father, but then she saw Humphrie peering at Bayard's back left foot.

"Is something wrong?"

"He's missing a nail, 'tis fine for short journeys, but if ye plan any distance he should go to the farrier."

"Do ye have time to do that today? I need to ride to Wardour tomorrow."

"I'll take him down there as soon as I'm finished here." Humphrie moved his head so that his eyes, the same colour as his brother's, looked straight into Anne's. "I saw that missing nail yesterday, when I cleaned his hooves. They were covered in unusual mud – I reckon it came from Purbeck."

Anne's hands tensed as she realised that the ostlers must know more than anyone, apart from Lizzie and Robert, about where she went on Bayard. She wondered whether to make up some story, but instead decided that since they knew so much, it was best to tell the truth, even if not all of it. "I went to

Corfe. I needed some help from the pirates there."

Humphrie smiled. "Ye need not worry, Mistress Anne," he said softly, "everyone in the stables knows that ye respects us and what we do, and even helps out when ye can. None of us has ever said a word to anyone, not even," and he gave her a wink, "when good Bayard came back from Dorchester with scorch marks on his flank!"

Anne replied with a broad smile, just as there came a clatter of hooves on cobbles. Through the stable doors, she glimpsed a horseman arriving, his doublet so torn and filthy no livery could be discerned. Curious, she put down her comb and went outside. The rider came to a halt in the courtyard and rather than dismounting, he fell off the side of his horse and would have crashed to the ground if Humphrie had not run up and caught him in his arms.

The ostler arranged the horseman half-lying on the ground, his back propped against a sack, and gave him small beer from a leather gourd, which he downed in great gulps.

Through the sweat and filth on his face, Anne recognised him as one of the men from Mistress Munday's tavern. His voice cracked and low, he said, "Mistress Anne. I have a letter, for thee, from the Captain," and he reached into his muddy doublet and drew out a flat leather purse.

"A letter? From the Captain?" Anne said, her heart beating hard.

She opened the pouch and took out a piece of the cheap parchment, which she recognised as the type used by traders in Dorchester market. But the writing was of the finest and for a moment Anne was bemused by this unexpected skill of the Captain's, until she realised that he must have paid a scrivener to write it for him.

"*Mistress Anne*," she read out, "*I made the trade with the black-clad man, and he took the gold. We shook hands and the deal was done.*" Anne guessed that the black clothes must refer to those worn by the executioner, and for a moment wondered why Heynes had used such a strange phrase, until she realised that he did not want the scrivener to know what he was doing. "*But later that day...*" She paused, suddenly aware of a total silence all around her. Realising that Humphrie and two small boys were listening, she continued reading quietly to herself, '*...he sent word that the gold is not enough. He has heard of your pearls and he wants those, and he swears thee must give them to him in person. I told him that he must honour his first promise, but his mind is made up...*"

Anne felt as though the cobbles of the courtyard were disintegrating under her, dropping her into a great void beneath. Her plans, she realised, were in ruins. Chidiock would die – the execution was just two days away, she could never get the pearls to London in time.

She looked up and saw that everyone was still staring at her. Taking a deep breath to steady herself, she said, "'Tis nothing … the Captain had promised more fabric for our kirtles but cannot buy it, we will have to find some from elsewhere." She looked at the horseman on the ground, who seemed to be sitting up straighter now that he had emptied the gourd, and said, "I thank ye, good master, for riding so hard, ye got here far quicker than I might have imagined."

The horseman put the gourd down and looked at her. "I had luck on the road, I was exhausted but I met a fine man with his lady, they helped me when I told them of the urgency to bring ye the Capn's message about pearls."

Anne felt an unpleasant sensation in her stomach at the thought of strangers being told about the pearls, but she just said, "Then, Fortune was on our side, and I thank ye again." She turned and hurried into the house, one arm across her face to hide the dampness that was welling up, the other clutching the letter.

She found Lizzie polishing pewter in the parlour. "Please, bring it with thee, I will help, but I need to show you this letter."

They went upstairs and Anne sat on her bed, beckoning Lizzie to sit beside her, where she leant on the maid's shoulder and handed her the leather purse, tears flooding out and still not saying a word. Lizzie took the letter and read out loud, slowly but clearly, first the part that Anne had already seen, and then continuing: "*... And there is other news: all London is saying that thy brother Henry is to be tried next week and will meet the same fate as Chidiock. They say young Arundell sits in his house at Westminster and arranges this.*"

"William? Arranges this!" Anne was almost shouting and she stood up abruptly, wiping her tears away with one hand as she grabbed the letter with the other, ripping the corner off it. "So this was why he went to London! How dare he! He promised to help by delaying Henry's trial, and now he seems to accelerate it!"

"There are two more sentences that I haven't read yet, maybe there's something there."

Anne gripped the letter roughly as she read, "*Stephen, who brings this to ye, is a good man but he cannot fly, and nor can thee, so I fear we have no time. But I have been becalmed before now without hope of escape, and then the wind changed suddenly, so in case fortune lends ye a horse with wings, I will wait for ye and thy jewels at the jetty on the Southwark shore below the bridge, from dusk till midnight on the 19th.*"

Anne's eyes were shining bright. "I will go! Now, within the hour! Not to Wardour, but to London!"

Lizzie, still sat on the bed, looked up at her. "There is no chance! You would need to be there tomorrow night! The nineteenth is tomorrow, how can you hope to arrive so soon? 'Tis two full days' ride, if not three. And there may be bad men on the road, there may be storms..."

Anne held the parchment high above her head, waving it in the air. "I remember when we were delayed at the weir and I thought it was too late to save Grandma, but Christopher said, 'True hope is swift!' With prayers to God and the help of Bayard, I will take the pearls to the executioner to save Chidiock – and the parchment to William, to save Henry!"

Lizzie stood up, and looked Anne in the eyes, speaking softly. "Those are thy Grandma's pearls, she gave them to thee, to have for thy wedding."

"She gave them to me to do as I saw best," said Anne, speaking low but without hesitation. "The Lady Elizabeth was a great woman and she would counsel me to act like this, if she was here."

"But what of the danger?" Lizzie was frowning deeply as she spoke. "Bribing an executioner is surely a crime – and while gold can come from any man, those pearls are known to everyone, there is none like them in the whole of England."

"The executioner is not going to take them to the Justices, his own head would be forfeit. He will sell them in some dark way, to protect himself, and by so doing, he will protect me. And if he does not – I will deal with that when it happens, and meanwhile, Chidiock will have been saved. As will Henry, if I find William and make him stick to his promise!" She squeezed Lizzie's hands. "I must go and tell the ostlers to prepare Bayard – and check that the missing nail has been replaced."

As Anne came down the stairs and went into the Screens Passage, there was a rustle in the curtains opposite and Gyb slid through, followed by Ma Melemouth, who slipped between the drapes as silently as her cat. "I heard ye had an urgent message from London," she said, looking at Anne.

"Yes," said Anne, "both Chidiock and Henry are facing new dangers, I have to go there to help them."

"What can a young girl like thyself do, that a grown man cannot?"

"I..." Anne hesitated, before continuing, "I have to give someone my pearls. And someone else a parchment. Only I can do it."

"Those pearls!" said Ma Melemouth, and her face seemed to Anne to become even more lined than usual. "I told ye that Young John meant only harm by giving them to ye – and that remains true, even now he is dead."

Anne gasped. "He is dead?"

"Aye, he passed away this morning, God rest his soul."

Anne was silent for a moment, and then she said, "May God rest his soul, but I will not pray for him." She found herself wanting to break out into a broad grin, but she stopped because she knew that was wrong, and could feel Ma Melemouth's eyes drilling down deep into her own.

"I doubt not," the crone said, "that as he lay on his sickbed, he plotted and planned to use those pearls to hurt ye. And he is succeeding already – thy hopes were raised that ye could enjoy wearing them, perhaps encourage some nice suitor. But now, ye must give them up – thy hopes are dashed!"

"I care not for some silly man who just wants me for my pearls!"

"That is not the only thing. If ye now give them to someone that ye should not, that can only lead to trouble."

Anne was silent for a moment, unsure what to say, but after a moment she said, "I've made my mind up. It's disappointing to give the pearls away, and maybe it's dangerous. But that's my choice, to save Chidiock."

Ma Melemouth stared at her silently for a moment, then reached into the folds of her old black dress, pulled out a piece of parchment, folded as a letter, and pushed it into Anne's hands. "If ye must go, then take this. Thy father penned it for Jane to use on her first trip to London, but she went with two strong servants and had plenty of time, so she never needed it. Take it and use it when ye is pressed."

The old crone shuffled away, Gyb beside her, and Anne looked at the letter. It was addressed to Baron Dacre, Chelsea, and sealed in red wax with the stamp of the Martyn's Ape. She could not read it without breaking the seal, and anyway there was no time with the light about to fade, so she shoved it into her pocket and hurried down to the stables.

Chapter 16

Red Sky at Night

Great streaks of reds and crimsons split the dark blue sky from north to south. Standing outside the stables with his hand on Bayard's halter, Humphrie said to Anne, "We will have Bayard saddled and ready for ye in a few minutes. And I've sent word to the farrier, he is ready for ye, and will do that missing nail when ye pass by his workshop. 'Twill take barely a moment."

He led Bayard into the stables, and Anne went over to Lizzie, who had come to say her farewells, and said, "Red sky at night, shepherd's delight: the weather will be good tomorrow."

"But it will be cloudy tonight. Is there no chance to wait till the morrow?"

"I cannot. Even Bayard would not get to London in a single day. I have to leave now, and cover thirty miles before finding an inn for the night." She started shivering, and squeezed her hands into fists to stop it showing, as she thought of other dangers that she did not even want to discuss. Sleeping in a strange inn was an act of foolhardiness for a lone maid. If she survived that, she had to ride further in a day than most men would in three, then somehow find the executioner in London.

Anne looked at Lizzie and suddenly knew what she wanted to do. She took out the little box from her inner pocket and pressed it into the maidservant's palm. "Lizzie, only God knows what will happen to me on this journey. So this is a keepsake from me to you, it came from my grandmother Joan, I meant to give it to you on the day of thy betrothal, but everything was so confused by the news about the arrests."

Lizzie took the little box and for a second Anne thought she might hand it back, but she opened it and looked at the opal necklace, and then did something quite different.

"In my room, I have a small bracelet from my Grandmama, a tiny one, 'tis from a poor woman and I'm sure worth nothing, but it will be my gift to you."

"Lizzie, that will be the most valuable thing I will ever have."

Humphrie appeared, leading Bayard, now saddled. From the road there came a roaring noise and Sir Nicholas and Sir George thundered up,

coming to a halt beside Anne, Urian leaping beside them barking loudly. The two men jumped to the ground and threw their reins to the waiting ostlers, sweat glistening from their brows. They had clearly been at the hunt and both were in as good a mood as Anne had seen.

"Well met!" her father cried. "I hope ye have had as fine sport riding Bayard as we had in the woods!" Her mind full of robbers waiting in the shadows on the road, but trying as hard as she could to keep the fear from wetting her eyes, she replied: "He has proved to be a mount that even a queen could pine for."

Her father's companion looked at her closely. "If what I hear is true, Bayard has already rendered ye great service. But what of today? Here is Bayard saddled, surely ye is not setting out as the light fades?"

Anne paused. Could she make up some story? But Bayard was here, ready with the saddlebags worn for a long journey. She took a deep breath and said, "I...I have to go to Westminster, to the Arundells' town-house. I have a document that may be able to save Henry, it has to be given to William, only I can do it. I must be there by dusk tomorrow evening." Knowing her father's views about bribery, she didn't mention that apart from seeing William, she must complete an even more urgent task: taking the pearls to the executioner.

Her father looked at her with astonishment and said, "'Tis impossible. The sun will be down within barely an hour, the ride to London takes a grown man two full days, a maid would take longer and the dangers are beyond all reason!"

Sir George was nodding. "Aye, let us go in the morning, we will ride with ye. If this document can really save Henry, it matters not whether it is tomorrow or three days hence, there is no talk yet of putting him on trial, that will come after poor Chidiock is gone."

Anne dug her fingernails into her palms in frustration, for Sir George was already indicating to Humphrie to take Bayard away, while her father put his arm on her shoulder, gently starting to nudge her towards the house.

Tears welling in her eyes, she looked back at Bayard, and saw both Humphrie and Lizzie pointing at Bayard's back left foot, whispering to one another. She shook her head to show incomprehension, as they pointed more urgently. Suddenly she understood.

She said to her father, "I...I must be ready for the morning, Bayard is missing a nail, the farrier is all ready to do the job, I must go there."
Sir Nicholas frowned. "The ostlers can arrange that for thee."

"I...Bayard is so special for me, I have only just started riding him...it may be strange, but I like to watch such work myself."

Sir George put his hand on Sir Nicholas' arm and laughed. "Let her go. 'Tis good that a rider takes care to understand a new mount."

Sir Nicholas nodded. "'Tis true. Go, but hurry there and back, for ye must to bed early tonight, to be ready to start at dawn."

Chapter 17

The Upright Man

The remnants of a great log glowed bright and warm in the fireplace, Anne sitting to one side and two fine ladies on the other. She was blushing, not from the warmth of the fire, but from the deceit she had practised on her father and Sir George. After the missing nail had been replaced, she had not gone back to Athelhampton, but had turned Bayard's head to the London road. It had been difficult to see in the gloaming, and in one place where the trees crowded in and hid such light as remained in the sky, she'd misjudged a bend and had pulled Bayard round only just in time. But at last, in almost complete darkness, she had reached the Albion tavern at Wimborne.

This is a different world from the inn at Corfe, she thought, looking at the delicate carving on the wooden benches, the well-dressed landlady behind the bar and the spotless stone floor. The two ladies had made polite conversation, accepting without question her explanation for travelling alone due to having arrived a day early for a meeting with her sister. The only other customers in the inn were two men dressed in the livery of some noble house, talking quietly in the corner. Anne thought how right Mistress Munday had been to tell the Captain to scrub up before coming here, and how wise he had been to avoid it altogether.

She pulled from her pocket the letter that Ma Melemouth had given her. Who was Baron Dacre? An image of a silver bracelet came to her mind. For a moment she could not understand why, and then she remembered that she was trying it on in Dorchester market just after she heard Baron Dacre's name for the first time. She studied the seal: most of it was attached to one fold of the parchment, so she could open it by making just a small tear on the other fold. It was a less obvious way to open the letter than by breaking the wax.

She read it to herself:

Dacre,
The bearer is my daughter Jane.
She is on the most urgent business for me and I
commend her to you.
Pray give her all assistance that she commands
of whatever kind.
With my deepest thanks,
Nicholas Martyn

As she read, she thought: 'Why has Ma Melemouth given this to me? It refers to Jane, so I can't use it. And though I know that Chelsea is just before London, I don't know exactly where. And anyway, someone as eminent as a Baron is not going to want to help me meet a pirate at some dark jetty on the Thames.'

She shoved the letter back into her pocket, and went upstairs to bed.

Aside from the distant noise of a buzzard's wings, Anne could hear only the sound of Bayard's breathing. She smiled at its strength and steadiness, despite the four hours taken mostly at a canter since leaving the Albion at dawn. A gleam of sunlight on stone caught her attention through the trees, and far away to her left and well behind her, she glimpsed a tall spire. "Winchester Cathedral!" she said out loud, and her smile broke into a grin as she added, "I'm glad we passed that by, good Bayard! 'Tis a place likely to be frequented by Walter Bearde's men."

She turned to look forward, and saw a cluster of pretty cottages nestling around a stone-built church and a small river. This must be Abbotstone, she thought, the last of the small villages on the route recommended by the innkeeper as a way to avoid the city. As she rode between the buildings, a whiff of fresh bread wafted out from an open door where a mother stood with her children, and she returned their wave without slackening pace. Beside the church a dark-clad man was hauling a black flag with a white cross up a flagpole.

Anne frowned as she rode past the last of the houses and up a hill, thinking, ''Tis an odd symbol to fly near a holy house.' But there was rivulet beside the track that her mount could drink from, and the smell of baking in her nose was reminding her that she had not eaten since leaving the inn. She came to a halt and took out the provisions given to her by the landlady, saying out loud, "Ye deserve some water, good Bayard, we can pause for a moment. That flag is likely nothing more than the arms of some local squire."

She tore off a great hunk of bread and stuffed it into her mouth with a slice of beef, realising how ravenous the riding had made her. ''Tis not very ladylike,' she thought, smiling, 'but there is no-one here to see me, so I can do what I want!' Across the vista of the rolling downland surrounding her, there was a glint of light from a clump of trees in the valley below her. She peered at it for a moment, and choked on her food as she realised there were mounted men, almost invisible save when sunlight caught the metal of their stirrups.

'Perhaps there is an innocent reason why men wait, hidden, in a copse,' she thought, 'but I doubt it, especially after seeing that unusual flag. Could it be Walter and his men?' Her hands started to tremble, and she dropped some of the bread as she shoved the uneaten remains of her meal back into her pouch.

Two men emerged from the trees, dressed in black, and started to ride rapidly along the bottom of the valley. She looked ahead and saw that her hilltop trail gradually descended and eventually met theirs – they were planning to get to the junction before her! She looked over her shoulder and saw a third man a few hundred paces behind on her own track, and felt a chill spreading down her spine as she realised that she could not go back, and with a steep drop on either side of her, there was no choice other than to go forward, and hope to outrun all the riders.

As Bayard surged forward, Anne looked down. The two men in the valley were riding at speed along a sheep-track, which ran parallel to a fast-moving stream. Her hands went cold as she realised that they wore fearsome long swords.

Looking ahead, she saw that just before the two tracks met, they each passed through narrow gateways in a high stone wall. Whoever rode through their gateway first would win the race to the junction. Her heart thumped as she guessed that she was a thousand paces from the wall, the two men barely half that.

A shout came from the valley below. "Drop the pearls, good mistress!" She felt herself burning with anger at the thought that Walter or his men had heard of her mission and were trying to foil it by seizing the pearls, and she urged Bayard forward even faster as they cried, "Drop them, and we will let thee go free!"

She was gaining on the men, but not enough to stop them cutting her off at the ford. Her heart beat louder than the wind at the thought of what they would do if they caught her, and she found herself glancing down at the pocket where the pearls were hidden, wondering whether she should be sensible and throw them on the ground. But an image came to her mind of Jane at Almer, talking of her love for Chidiock, and she remembered the promise she had made to save him. She squeezed her feet into Bayard's flanks and cried out, "No! I will surrender nothing to those who threaten a poor maid!"

"Then we will take the pearls, and cut thee for the carrion to eat!"

She could see the men more clearly now; they rode beside one another, the one nearer to her finely dressed in a coat of good black velvet which must have cost more than a horse – he was clearly the leader.

The gap in the wall on their side of the stream was barely a hundred paces ahead of them, hers twice that – any hope of outpacing them was gone. She saw the face of her mother, sympathising over scratches when she'd fallen from a tree aged six, and tears welled up as she tensed herself for the blows of their swords.

Squeezing her eyes, she looked ahead and realised that the gaps in the stone wall were narrower than seemed from afar, barely enough for a single rider, and she realised what she had to do. "Never!" she cried, "'tis ye who will feel the Bridport dagger!" He shouted a bad word in response, and Anne cried again, "I know fine men to weave that good rope into a fair noose for ye and thy friends!"

An even fouler word came back and Anne let out a great sigh of relief, as she saw that her stratagem had worked. The well-dressed man had been too busy yelling at her to order his companion to pull back. Now, they both had to rein in sharply, for they could not pass through the gap together. She heard him cry to his fellow, "Let me ahead, curse you!" but they had lost momentum and must slow almost to a halt, before one could pass through in front of the other.

Bayard swept through their gap in the wall without slackening pace, crossed the river by a ford and galloped up the hill beyond. Anne looked back at the two villains from the valley; by the time they had got through the narrow gate and regained speed, they were several hundred paces behind her. The third man, who had been on the same track as her, had now caught up with them.

Anne's breathing quickened as she saw the sweat across Bayard's flanks – it reminded her that he had been riding swiftly for many hours with only the briefest pauses, while her pursuers had been lying in wait for her, so their mounts had been resting. Her lead was enough for now, but at the pace they were moving, even Bayard would start to tire, and then the men could catch up.

She looked for some place of refuge, but up on these high hills there were no houses; and anyway, the three thieves behind her would rapidly subdue any poor farmer. She needed to find a noble house, but had no idea where one was.

Her gaze travelled across the fields, populated only by sheep, longing for the strong stone houses near Winchester that she had passed when the sun was still low in the sky. An invisible memory was tapping a corner of her mind, like a friend in a game of hide and seek, telling her that the name of that great city was important, but she could not recall why – Friar Wytterage had sometimes mentioned it in lessons about the great Cathedrals, but what use was that?

Then she remembered the Great Hall at Wardour, and Sir George's comment about William's kinsman, who '...lived well beyond Winchester...' on the way towards London. Any relative of William's must surely have a fine house! She leaned forward and cried into Bayard's ear, "To Sutton Place!"

Bayard swung his great head to the right, jumped easily over the tumbledown remains of a low stone wall into a field, scattering sheep to either side. Behind, Anne heard laughter and the rasping cry of the elegantly-attired thug, "Ye'll not escape us that way, young mistress," and she heard the thump of hooves following her. They started up a steep hill and Bayard's pace slowed, confirming her fears about his tiredness, and her hands went cold as she heard shouts behind, "We have her now!"

They went into woods, where in the half-light amidst the leaves a branch caught Anne's sleeve as though trying to tug her out of the saddle, and there was a tearing sound as a strip of material was ripped from her riding-kirtle. They came out of the trees into the light of a valley; on the horizon smoke rose from the chimneys of a fine house set in a great park, but it was protected by a high wall, a tall iron gate and a lodge, in front of which stood a man in livery holding an ancient flintlock, which he raised to his shoulder and pointed at her.

"Ye must help me, not shoot me!" She was screaming, and could taste the salt from her tears. "I'm a friend of William Arundell!" She was barely fifty paces from the gate as she heard the crash of breaking branches behind her, signalling that the robbers were emerging from the woods, and again she cried out, "I'm being chased by villains!"

Without warning, there was a great noise as the lodge-keeper fired his piece, and Anne tensed herself for the pain. None came, and glancing back she saw that it had stirred up a great cloud of stone and dust in front of her pursuers, whose mounts swerved to avoid it. The keeper opened the postern and gasping with relief she rode through, bringing Bayard to a halt behind the lodge while the gate was swung shut behind her. There was a click as her guardian reloaded; he called out, "Stand back, leave, the next is aimed at thy heart!" and Anne felt her breathing ease as the sound of hooves retreated into the distance.

The keeper came round the side of the lodge, laughing. "They're the greatest cowards ever, they run like rabbits as soon as they're faced with a gun – and they will not catch ye now, for ye can take the short way through the park, while they must ride all the way round the walls."

Bayard was drinking from a stone trough, while Anne, dismounted, doused her face and neck with water from the nearby pump and gulped the cool liquid into her mouth, unmindful as it splashed onto her collar.

The keeper gave her a quizzical gaze. "Ye have been riding hard to escape those villains, good mistress – 'tis strange they pursue a young maid, they usually they target rich men."

"'Tis strange, indeed." Anne looked up and found she had to squeeze her hands into fists to stop herself shaking, for the man's eyes were narrowing as he stared at her.

"Ye is a friend of Lord Arundell, my master's cousin? Thy luck is out, for he left for London a few days back, my master with him." The keeper moved towards her as he spoke.

"'Tis no matter, I will meet him there. I must be on my way." Anne put her foot in the stirrup and swung her leg across the saddle.

The keeper was now a pace away. "Afore ye go: Lord Arundell's servant said some interesting things about a young maid, name of Anne. It's been the talk of everyone below stairs, ever since."

Anne felt a chill from the wet collar of her kirtle. "What did he say?"

"'Twas 'bout some fine jewels of hers. Good enough for a Queen, he said. Is thy name Anne, perchance?" She began to shiver all over, as the man put his hand out to grab the bridle.

But Bayard turned his head sharply, shifting it out of reach. Anne pulled hard on the reins and they moved swiftly away, towards the neat paths of the park, leaving her inquisitor far behind.

The sun had been below the horizon for nearly an hour as Bayard picked his way sluggishly along the road, the last of the daylight glinting dully off the waters of the Thames beside them. Anne could see her mount's muscles pulsating through the dried sweat that coated his mane, and she tensed her limbs to keep herself awake and upright in the saddle. They were moving more slowly than on a trip with Jinty to collect acorns, and Anne could feel despair creeping over her, like the tendrils of ivy eating away the mortar of a wall, as she began to realise that neither she nor Bayard had the strength to make the remaining miles to London.

"Dear Bayard, we have come so far, I think it must be a hundred miles, but we have no energy left, and the dark is closing in." They came to a complete halt, and with Bayard's hooves no longer clip-clopping on the stony track, the only noise Anne could hear was the faint splashing of the river water, stirred by some boat invisible in the twilight. She waited, hoping that a moment's rest might revive her, but her eyes fell shut and she started to fall sideways out of the saddle, and had to heave herself upright.

In the near-silence, a tiny, distant sound became audible: faint voices, excited and laughing. It's probably a party, thought Anne, which meant there was a big house somewhere, and she remembered the letter to Baron Dacre. Could his house be nearby? Dare she use a letter with Jane's name? It was one thing to be squeamish about using it in the warm brightness of the Albion Inn, and quite another here in the cold darkness beside the river.

She felt a sudden surge of hope, as energising as the Captain's hot brown liquid, and she leaned forward and said, "To Baron Dacre's house," praying that Bayard would know it, and that it was close enough to reach before they both collapsed from exhaustion.

Bayard moved forward, and he seemed to go slower and slower and the darkness become even more intense, and Anne had to squeeze her eyes to stop herself crying at the thought that she was going to fail.

She slowly became aware that the rough bushes to her left had given way to a well-made brick wall, and the voices she had heard earlier were now more distinct. Bayard's pace increased slightly and she sat up straighter, all thoughts of sobbing banished. Ahead, by the light of torches, she saw two great barges moored on the riverside. A group of elegantly-dressed ladies and gentlemen stepped out from them and passed through a gateway in the wall lit either side by burning braziers.

Anne caught her breath – would a young girl in a dusty kirtle on a mud-stained mount be admitted amidst these glittering Londoners? But she had to try, and Bayard seemed confident that they were entering the right place, for he tugged gently against her grip to turn in through the gates. They followed the fashionable crowd up a short gravelled path to a great stone house, where a doorman, in ochre and crimson livery, stared at her torn clothes and sweaty horse and said in a sneering tone, "And who may I...announce?"

Anne sat up straight in her saddle and looked

down at him, drawing out the letter from her pocket. "You may take this letter to my Lord Dacre," she said, "and then find stabling for my horse and somewhere that I may make clean after journeying."

She had barely had time to brush the worst of the dust off her kirtle in a small room near the entrance, when a knock on the door announced the arrival of a liveried footman. "My Lord will see you at once," he said, bowing so deeply that Anne at first wondered whether he might overbalance, and then she thought, 'This footman is so much more polite than the gatekeeper, it must be because they've read Father's letter!'

She was shown into a great chamber, tapestries hanging on every wall in between high glass windows, with candles burning bright and a great fire even on this summer's evening. As she entered, an old man stood up and came across to her. He was stooped and barely came to her shoulder.

Anne curtseyed low and he responded with a slow bow, saying, "Mistress Jane, most welcome. I trust you had a good journey."

She felt herself breaking into a sweat. In the excitement of finding the house and entering the haven of warm and well-lit rooms, she had put the deception out of her mind. Now she had to decide: would she pretend to be Jane, or take the risk of telling the truth?

"I...I'm Anne. Jane is my sister. She didn't need the letter, so I borrowed it." She could not breathe, as the Baron looked at her silently, and she imagined him throwing her out, or telling the nasty doorman to lock her up.

But he burst out laughing. "Ah, I see that the Martyn daughters are as resourceful and bold as the rest of the family! Thy relatives have done me great favours in the past, and it matters not to me whether ye be Jane or Anne – though I hope also to make thy sister's acquaintance in the future."

A servant offered a tray with dark red wine in a large engraved glass and a tankard of small ale and Anne seized the latter, trying to be elegant as she slaked her thirst from it. "And now, you must tell me about your journey – you look to have come a long way."

"Indeed yes," said Anne, "I came from Wimborne this morning, and the ride was good, save for a hill this side of Winchester, where some men with a well-dressed leader chased me."

The Baron's polite smile gave way to a deep frown. "We call that type of thief an Upright Man. He dresses as a gentleman, but his trade is thuggery. Such a man often works with a lady who also dresses well, but is as bad as he is. I will alert the Justices to track him down." Anne was reminded of the 'fine man with his lady' who in helping Heynes' messenger had found out about her and the pearls – he must have been the leader of the villains, rather than Walter being involved.

Dacre was was continuing. "Now, I understand you need assistance. Everything I have is at your disposal." He leaned forward. "Your grandmother's spouse, Old Sir John Tregonwell, persuaded our good Queen to restore to me the title that had been taken away from my father. Nothing I can do would fully repay such a debt, but I will do what I can, and," his voice fell even further, so that Anne had to lean forward to hear, "you can trust to my total discretion, whatever it is you have to do."

Anne smiled with relief, as she realised that she could ask the Baron for anything, despite his great nobility. She said, "I need to visit the Arundells' mansion. And after that, I must reach a certain jetty, just beyond London Bridge, before midnight."

The old man looked at her. "I will arrange whatever you wish. But my advice, if you wish for it, would be to abandon the Arundells, and go straight to the jetty. My watermen can take you there directly on my private barge, 'tis little over an hour, past Westminster Abbey and the royal palace. There is a cabin where you can rest and change, for my dear daughter, Mary, is of thy size, and I am sure will willingly give you fresh clothes. Your fine horse can be fed and rested and delivered overnight to wherever you wish – if ye go to London Bridge, I recommend the George Inn, 'tis close by there and is the best lodging in London."

"My Lord," said Anne, "I am deeply grateful for your counsel, which I take most seriously, but may you tell me why you say this about the Arundells?"

Anne found herself being stared at closely as the Baron said, "There are rumours…" He paused, before continuing, "…rumours circulating in London. That is not such an unusual thing, and often they have no substance. Still, one should be careful."

"Rumours?" said Anne. "About what?"

The old man looked at her closely again, before saying, "They refer to you, or at least, to a Martyn daughter, which I suppose might mean one of your sisters, but I think it is you."

"To me?" said Anne. "What do they say?" and she felt the blood racing through her heart as he replied.

"They say that the young Arundell, William, has plans to arrest you and take you to the Tower."

Chapter 18
The Executioner

"Don't look up there, young mistress," the Baron's waterman advised, as he helped her off the beautiful Dacre barge. This had bought her down the river in the comfort of a cushioned stateroom, all the way from Chelsea, past the great towers of Westminster Abbey, and was now moored just upstream of the great London Bridge. "That's where they end up, 'em that plots against Her Majesty."

Anne, however, could not resist looking up, and immediately felt her supper starting to rise up from her belly. Almost directly above them, on the gate that gave access to the bridge from Southwark, were a series of human heads, just visible in the lantern light. She quickly looked away and gave a silent prayer for the departed souls.

"Follow me across here," her escort said, leading her onto a street busy with carts, horses and roughly-dressed men and women, the clash of wheels on cobbles almost deafening. For a moment Anne thought they would turn onto London Bridge itself, but he took her straight across the road and down a narrow alley lit only by a single rushlight. With one hand she lifted her kirtle above her ankles to keep it out of the dirty water that seemed to be everywhere,

and with the other she pinched her nose tight shut against its stench. The way descended and ahead, between tall buildings, she caught a glimpse of lights reflecting on the river.

"We left the river and climbed up, and now we are going back down to it! Why are we coming this way on foot?" she asked, her hands suddenly cold in the London night air. Might the Baron's man prove as treacherous as the lodge keeper at Sutton Place? "We could just have taken the barge under the bridge!"

The waterman gave a chuckle. "Not if you want to stay good and dry, young mistress. The space between the piers of old London Bridge is barely wide enough for the Baron's fine boat, and the current there is treacherous. 'Tis not far now."

Ahead, Anne saw a wooden jetty, an open rowing boat, and five silhouettes against against the lights of the quayside buildings. Her breathing came faster as she saw a hand move to a jewelled hilt, and heard boots on timber as one of the figures stepped towards her. A voice came from the murk: "Ye do indeed have wings, to get here tonight."

Anne's breathing slowed. "Well met, Captain Heynes."

"Good morrow, mistress Anne. Are ye ready to meet this foul executioner?"

"All is ready," said Anne, her hand on the bulge in her pocket where the pearls were concealed.

Plumed hat in hand, the Captain bowed, now close enough to be seen, and said, "'Twill take some while, let us go now."

The Baron's waterman made his own bow to Anne, and disappeared into the night, and she stepped towards the rowing boat. The villain nearest to her put his hand out towards her and she pulled away from him, but the Captain gave a low laugh and said, "Ye have no need to fear Bosun Munday, he is my oldest shipmate and a good man to have in any fight. He is just helping thee onto the boat."

They pushed away from the jetty into the river, and Anne caught a glimpse of tall masts of moored ships silhouetted against the gibbous moon, but they slipped past only slowly and after a few minutes she said, "Where are we going? We seem to make little headway."

"We go to the Devil's Tavern," said Heynes, "'tis over on the Wapping side, but we fight the tide, so we go downstream in the shallows and then cross back."

"The executioner is there?" Anne asked.

"Aye," came the reply, "'tis a place for outlaws and thieves, ordinary folk do not care for headsmen, so needs must he drinks there."

As the oars splashed, the Captain spoke quietly into Anne's ear. "I had my men find out where thy sister Jane lodges – she is at the George Inn. 'Tis the best bed in town, and better still, 'tis but a few hundred paces from the jetty where we met. After we have done our work, I can take thee there – I sent her word that ye might be coming."

"That is good news," said Anne, "especially good, for that is where Bayard has been sent."

The boat gave a sharp bump, and though little was visible in the dark, Anne guessed they had reached the far side of the river. "These Wapping steps are coated with a thicker slime than on the other side," said the Captain. "It helps the customs men slip and saves the labour of dispatching them."

The Captain's hand, thought Anne, gripping it tight to keep balance, had not shied from the work of finishing a fair few men, but she kept her peace. Then she was safe ashore, a stench too foul to name, the street lined with warehouses so tall they hid the moonlight, the only illumination a hundred paces ahead where a painted pelican hung under a flaming torch.

"This is the sign of the inn," said Heynes, pointing, "I know not why."

The tavern was more disgusting than anything Anne could imagine, and made the inn at Corfe look like a palace. It was not just that the stench was sickening and the building ramshackle, with chickens running wild. At Mistress Munday's, there had been excitement and merriment in every corner, but here were the drinkers were morose, the smell was of rotting food, the illumination no more than a pair of feeble rushlights. As Anne looked at the elegance of her gown in the midst of this filth, she felt almost regal and she stood as tall as she could, checking that the dark crimson folds were neat from her shoulders to her ankles and saying a silent thanks to the Baron's daughter Mary for insisting on the best Huguenot silk. The Captain was about to enter ahead of her, but she signed him aside. Her mother always went first when on a mission of command.

The talk faded as men became aware of her arrival, and the crowd parted to open a way to a stocky, bald man, his short leather jacket open to show the dark hair of his chest, his eyes already focused on hers. The executioner!

Anne felt a coldness running from her fingertips and up her arms to her heart, for this was no place for a girl, and she had to squeeze the muscles of her neck to suppress the almost overwhelming instinct to turn and check that the Captain and his men were still there to protect her.

An image of Jane and Chidiock, taking their betrothal vows on the lawn at Athelhampton, came into her mind and she pressed her hands into fists to banish the coldness, and to give herself the boldness to complete her mission. She stepped forward through the foul mess of liquid and chicken feathers splashed across the floor, and stopped a pace in front of the executioner.

"Send these men away," she said, the words from intuition more than plan, and only after they were spoken did she realise that a bribe cannot be given in front of a crowd. The executioner gave a small nod, and his companions started to move, slowly at first, and then he gave the man closest to him a shove and they were pushing and falling against one another in their haste to move away.

She took out the jewel-bag, but as she held it an image came into her mind. It was the great chamber at Mylton, with her grandma in front of the statues of King Athelstan and his bride, handing the necklace to Endy and asking him to count the pearls, before turning to her and saying, 'one day, when you are older, I will give this to you.' Her hand started to edge the bag back towards her pocket, her eyes dropped away from the executioner's face, and the whole inn was silent.

From behind her, she heard someone's breathing quicken – might it be the Captain's? The sound brought her mind back to the present and the image of Mylton vanished. She drew herself up to full height, lifted the bag and held it out to the bald man.

"You will not execute my brother tomorrow. You will show him mercy, and in recognition of this service, I give you this."

She thought: it is a command; I will not negotiate, not permit an inspection of the contents, that would break the spell; he must accept the terms as offered. She waited, wordlessly, suppressing any thought of what she would do if he refused or argued; every inch of her face must show that she knew he would do as she asked.

And then he was on his knee, bowing his head, and afterwards looking up at her as he took the bag. "It will be as you command, my lady. We 'ave tricks, pig's blood, a chicken that screams when we cut its throat, to make it seem that it's your brother in pain." She gave a tiny nod of her head, trying to copy the imperceptible movement she had seen her father make after passing judgement in cases between feuding farmers, for what was there for her to accept, when the executioner's agreement had never been in doubt?

And then she felt sick and just wanted to turn and run away, back to Bayard, back home, to her own room, away from this stench and horror, to lie quietly alone in her own bed under the blankets. But she could not just leave, and for a moment she felt the coldness creeping back into her fingertips, as she found herself quite unable to think how to end the exchange with this terrible man.

"Where will you take him, afterwards?" The familiar voice of the Captain, suddenly beside her, was like the warmth of sunlight on a cold morning. Of course, she realised, plans have to be made, and it would not be appropriate for her to be involved in such details. She took a step back, as the executioner spoke. "'Ee'll be brought to Blackfriars. 'Tis close to the gallows, from there ye can take a wherry down to the docks and pop 'im on a boat to wherever you want."

The Captain responded, "And you'll have another body, to take his place?"

The executioner gave a laugh that seemed to Anne more unpleasant than anything she'd heard even from Young John. "There's always a few corpses lying around these parts, and if we can't find one the right size, then we'll find someone who's still walking and use a rope and knife on 'em. Lots of people round 'ere who won't be missed if they disappear."

Anne's mouth fell open at this horror, and she was about to object, but the Captain nodded briskly at the executioner and turned to Anne. "'Tis done. I will take ye back to your sister."

She picked up her skirts, to keep them above the filth on the floor, holding herself up straight to look elegant and regal as she exited the hovel, but inside she wanted to curl up with Jane and cry with relief.

With the tide now helping them, the journey back across the Thames seemed to take barely a few minutes. Despite the coldness of the river air, Anne felt warm as she took the Captain's hand and stepped onto the jetty, for her mission was done and she was but a few hundred paces from the safety of the George Inn where Jane lodged.

"I thank ye, Captain," she said, "'tis a job well done."

"Aye," said Heynes, "but thee is not back to safety yet, let us go quietly, with the bosun ahead of us, for pickpockets and cut-purses make the road between the river and the George their own, and I would rather we heard them before they hear us."

They picked their way through the dark streets. Anne put one hand on Heynes' shoulder and the other to her mouth to stifle her cry as her foot went into a deep puddle of sticky filth, which gurgled as she pulled her leg out. Ahead was a single feeble light in a glass lantern hanging from the wall above head height. As they approached it, Anne saw that it marked a sharp bend in the lane, which was narrow and enclosed on both sides by high, windowless walls. Crouched under the light was a young boy, dressed in rags, but when he saw them he jumped up and raced away.

A figure appeared round the corner, and Anne was ready to shout a warning, until she saw it was the bosun, who came up to Heynes and whispered, "Four men-at-arms, guarding the entrance to the inn."

The Captain spat into the gutter. "That bodes ill. Maybe 'tis nothing to do with us, but we should take the back way."

Anne's hands went cold as she remembered the Baron's words about rumours. "Do you think they're there to arrest me? How could they know that I gave the executioner the pearls? It happened but a few minutes ago."

The Captain grunted. "These times are dangerous. Maybe 'tis me they seek – they could have discovered that Captain Heynes did not fall so deep into the water as they thought. Or, maybe 'tis ye. Either way, let us keep away from them."

"But if they really are a threat," said Anne, "what use is a back way into the inn? Once they know we're inside, they can just come in through the main gate and find us."

"Legally, they can come into an inn," said the Captain, "for only Church land is protected from them by law. But the George has its own guards, they will keep out everyone, unless they come with great force."

There seemed to be twists and turns every few paces, before at last Anne saw the bosun'un standing by a solid oak door in a high wall, lit by a single light, holding a bunch of keys.

"You have a key to this door?" asked Anne.
The bosun laughed. "I have a set of keys that will open any door on any ship, and taverns are much the same as ships." He tried three keys, and the fourth clicked in the lock and the door swung open.

Anne's breathing eased as she looked around at the great courtyard of the George Inn, full of carriages hunkered down for the night, emblazoned with the liveries of noble families. Twinkling candles lit the stairs that led up to the galleries, which ran round every wall to give access to the rooms. The Captain pointed quietly to a door two storeys up. "Jane is in that room up there."

The great wooden gates of the main entrance were closed tight shut, but within them, an inch ajar, was a small postern that gave access for latecomers. Anne saw that it was guarded by two armed watchmen, warming their hands on a brazier, and she started back until she saw they wore a black and red livery that matched the colours painted on the timbers of the inn.

As they crept past, Anne heard voices from outside, and recognising one, she stopped.

"Would thou wert clean enough to spit on! If I catch ye drinking ale again, ye will have a blow on the head to remember for the rest of thy miserable life!" The unpleasant growl of Walter Bearde was unmistakeable.

"But 'tis worrisome cold here, the ale will warm us till relief comes at dawn," said an unfamiliar voice.

"Ye need all thy wits about ye. This girl was seen by the lad I pay, just a few minutes ago. She may try to sneak in at any moment, disguised as a boy. That's what she does. She may be young but she's a traitor with two treacherous brothers in the Tower, she has a sly tongue and moves fast and ye must be ready to arrest her."

The chill flooded from Anne's hands to her heart, and though none could see through the narrow opening by the door, she drew her hood down right across her eyes and hurried past to reach the staircase to her sister's room.

Chapter 19

But a Frost of Cares

The light of a miserable morning squeezed past the closed shutters. "'Tis in the hands of God, now, dear sister," said Anne quietly as she eased a comb through Jane's auburn hair, "we can only pray that the executioner will honour the bargain."

"Whatever happens, I'm so grateful for all you have done. A sister's love matters so much in this terrible world of men with their plots and their knives. Even those who should help do not – Chidiock's commander, Sir Christopher, has done nothing, yet he's the Queen's favourite! And even Father did not want to bribe the executioner."

There was a knock at the door. Anne eased her sister's head off her lap and got up.

"Who's there?" She spoke through the closed door.

"A letter, from the Tower."

Anne opened the door, blinking at the daylight and trying to adjust her thoughts to the unfamiliar noises of the city. Outside on the narrow gallery stood a lad in a filthy leather jerkin, a great black bruise on one eye, behind him in the yard far below the ostlers shouting as they led horses between the gleam of newly polished carriages.

Anne took the parchment. It was rolled and tied

with a rough string, soiled from dirty hands, a scrawled word half hidden under his thumb.

"Thank 'ee, and here for your pains." Anne handed a coin from her pouch, from the lad's smirk it was too much, but what matter, she thought, on a day like this. She shut the door, brought the letter to Jane and lit the two candles, which to her surprise let a wonderful smell of beeswax into the room.

"Can this be for thee?" said Anne. "The name on it is Agnes!"

Anne saw a wan smile on her sister's drawn face. "'Tis the name Chidiock often uses for me when we are alone, it sounds so much like my name, and he says that 'tis the right name for me since it means Holy."

Jane took the parchment carefully, gently unrolling it and another smaller one inside. Anne, watching silently, saw her sister's deep, beautiful cat-green eyes open up and the smile spread across her angular face as she read aloud:

"My prime of youth is but a frost of cares
My feast of joy is but a dish of pain
My crop of corn is but a field of tares
And all my good is but vain hope of gain
The day is fled and yet I saw no sun
And now I live and now my life is done"

Jane was crying now. "I can read no more, dear sister. There are two more stanzas and then there is a letter to me, please take them, read me his last words."

Anne read the verses and the letter, shedding a

small tear of her own, and as she reached the end, she took her sister's hand.

"Do you have the strength to go?" said Anne, looking at her sister's flood of tears. "If we are to watch the executioner, now is the time." The candles were burning low, but still gave enough light for Anne to see Jane's emerald eyes fix on hers.

"'Twill be awful, with all these horrible people, but I wrote to Chidiock that I would be there."

"You will see him soon afterwards, the rendezvous is at Blackfriars. You do not have to be there."

"'But... just suppose this executioner does not honour his promise? I would never forgive myself if I was not there at Chidiock's last moments."

"He will honour it!" said Anne, but she squeezed her hands into fists as she spoke, for some tiny doubt still sat in her own mind.

"'Tis you, not me, I worry about," cried Jane, "for they say this William Arundell is to arrest you, and drag you to the Tower, I know not why. You should hurry to Blackfriars, and make ready to flee."

"Since you are going to the scaffold, I will come with you. I will not leave you to endure that horrid spectacle alone," and she took Jane's hands in hers and squeezed them tight. "But fear not, I will leave the George discreetly by a back way, so no-one will see to arrest me."

"Then I will come the same way!"

In the mud and bustle of the courtyard, an ostler, smart in the same black and red livery that the guards had worn the night before, had Bayard saddled and ready, a blanket thrown over him to hide the birthmark. Beside him was Jane's piebald.

Anne gave him a ha'penny, the right amount this time, and said, "Ye will meet us at the entrance to London Bridge. We will be there in ten minutes." She took Jane's hand and walked round the back of the yard to the postern gate that she had used the night before, and tapped on it. It was opened from the other side by the Captain and without a word they slipped through, following him along the maze of alleys and emerging at the arch with its terrible heads that marked the entrance to London Bridge. There, amidst the carters with sacks and barrels, women bare-headed and hooded, men in their fine clothes and their rags, was the ostler with Bayard and the piebald.

Anne looked round to check for any sign of Walter or his fellows. Heynes, who must have guessed what she was doing, laughed. "Those thuggish men-at-arms were still waiting for thee at the main gate when I went past a few minutes back. They will wait there all day! And now, I go to make arrangements for the ship. 'Twill be waiting at Blackfriars, to take ye, Mistress Jane, and Chidiock, to France."

The Captain bowed farewell and disappeared into the crowd, but Anne's eye had caught a glimpse of a small figure in familiar ragged clothes, racing back towards the inn. She felt her hands go cold on the reins as she realised it was the same lad who she'd seen the previous night. "They have spies," she said to Jane as they eased their horses into the flow of people headed across London Bridge, "and will be after us shortly."

"They will not be able to overtake us in this crush of people," replied Jane. "But once we reach the scaffold, they will not be far behind and will soon find us. Ye should go back home to Dorsetshire, and leave me to go on by myself – do not take risks where ye need not."

"I … It may seem madness, but I need to meet William," said Anne, "so if I see him at the scaffold, I will wait for him to come to me."

"No!" cried Jane. "That is madness indeed. Why should you allow yourself to be arrested?"

Anne's hands felt even colder as she gently eased Bayard through the crush of people, and she said softly, "I have to give him a parchment that may save Henry's life. I'm the only one who can do it."

Chapter 20

St Giles-in-the-Fields

Shuffling across London Bridge so slowly that they seemed to barely move, they reached a building chequered black and white that straddled the roadway, people crowding through its narrow gate. They inched forward, at last reaching the white-haired toll-keeper who took their ha'pennies and waved them through, but the crush did not abate and they had to keep halting. "Be watchful when we stop," said Jane, "for though the houses are noble and people wear fine clothes, there is plenty a cut-purse waiting in these side-alleys." Anne drew her riding-kirtle tighter around her, thinking that while the pouch concealed beneath carried no pearls, it did hold the five gold sovereigns that Baron Dacre had insisted on giving her for emergencies.

They never seemed to move more than a dozen paces before stopping, and after what seemed like an hour, Anne cried, "We have come no more than a thousand paces! How much further have we to go?"

"I believe at least another thousand."

"The I fear we will arrive too late, for we are not moving at all." She squeezed her face to block her nose, adding, "And we are stuck near some foul drain!"

"Folks call this the Fleet river."

"'Tis unlike any Dorsetshire stream! The stench is worse than the dung behind the stables!"

"We have no choice but to wait here till the crowd moves. There is no other route – I quizzed the doorman at the George last night."

"Let's ask Bayard." Anne spoke confidently, but she felt a tremor in her chest as she wondered whether her mount could possibly know the back-ways of London as well as he knew the roads of Dorsetshire and Hampshire. She bent forward and said, "Take us to St Giles-in-the-Field."

Bayard abruptly turned his head to the right, and inched through the crowd until he reached an almost deserted side-alley, leading away at right angles to the main road and parallel to the Fleet.

"Come," Anne cried, "come quick, for Bayard will fly, once he has space."

The passage was barely wide enough for a horse to pass a man, but the only people in it were an old lady scrubbing her laundry and two lads dicing. Bayard broke into a trot, barely inches from the high blank wall to their left.

The wall went on and on, and Anne heard Jane cry from behind "Where are we going? This leads us further and further from the main road!"

"Bayard has never taken me false before." Through a high iron gateway, Anne saw a sea of purple flowers and caught a strange and wonderful scent, so far distant from the foul stink of the sewer that it took her a moment to place it. "'Tis saffron, the owner must indeed be wealthy, Master Moryshe told me it costs more than gold."

"'Tis the palace of Sir Christopher, whose yeomanry Chidiock served in."

"Him!" Anne drew phlegm into her mouth to spit on the ground, as she'd seen men do at the mention of something bad, but swallowed it at the last minute as she remembered it was unladylike. "He did nothing to save Chidiock – he doesn't deserve to have this palace, not even a single thread of saffron!"

Three hundred paces on, Jane cried out. "Look ahead! This alleyway leads into another street where the crowd is as dense as before. I fear we may not pass."

But Bayard once more nudged gently through the people and reached the other side of the street. A slimy, cobbled ramp, occupied only by an old man leaning on his stick, descended to the waters of the Fleet river, and Anne realised that this was the way they would go. She readied herself for the stench of the river by trying to remember the saffron smell, but as Bayard splashed into the water, the air was clear.

"The smell here is fair! We are now upstream of that palace, and I'd wager that the steward there arranges a good beating for any man who tips what they should not into this part of the river."

"Fair-smelling this may be, yet I fear good Bayard knows London less well than Dorsetshire, for this river leads north, and far away from St Giles."

"I trust Bayard, and we have this route to ourselves."

They went slowly along the stoned and uneven river-bed for several hundred paces, until Bayard turned his dark head to the left and pushed between the overhanging branches of a great willow into a hidden side stream, narrow but running true and clear. They followed it, the water ever shallower, to the place where it ended under overhanging branches, a trickle from the mouth of a stone lion's head feeding the stream. Wide steps led up the bank and Bayard took Anne up these, Jane's piebald behind.

"We must now be close," said Anne.

"And William's men must be stuck in the crowds, so we will arrive well ahead of them!" They climbed the steps, then up a narrow and muddy track between tall bushes, and finally out to the top of an open hill.

Below them, the midday sun glinted on the Thames. The towers of the great abbey at Westminster stood tall in the distance, but much nearer, barely two hundred paces down the slope in front of them, was a small church – and beside it, the oaken horror of the scaffold. Anne swallowed to prevent herself from vomiting.

"We should dismount," said Jane, "otherwise William's men will see us as soon as they arrive."

Anne dragged her gaze to the crowds of people sitting and standing on the grass in front of them, and her nausea grew as she realised that everyone was waiting for Chidiock and his fellows to be butchered.

"Quickly," said Jane, and they dismounted, tethering the horses behind a bush as the crowd fell silent. Anne looked down the hillside to where the executioner, in black mask and hose, had appeared and was climbing the wooden steps up to the gallows, and this time she could not stop herself from retching.

Chapter 21
The Scaffold

As the first man was led to the scaffold, Anne shut her eyes and held out her hand to Jane, saying, "This is the sight we have come to see, and yet, 'tis the last thing in the world that I now want to watch."

There came a scream from below, and Anne tried not to listen, and then the crowd gave a roar that felt to her not like a group of men, but like some giant ogre, and she heard Jane say: "'Tis not him, 'tis his companion Babington, the man who led him into this, best we avert our eyes and close our ears," and Anne tried, but there below was a body writhing and screaming, and she looked away to the river, but then her gaze came back to the scaffold. And then at last, somehow, it was over.

"This is the stuff of which nightmares and demons are made, how can men do this to one another, and worse, how can men watch this, for sport?" said Anne.

"Men are hardened in war," said Jane, sobbing quietly, "and are hardened by the privations of life."

Anne squeezed her hand tighter. "In war, 'tis a fair fight, but this is butchery." She lowered her gaze again as another victim was led forward.

And then, after more horrors, she looked up

again, and caught a glimpse of that flaming red beard. "Look!" she whispered. "Now he comes."

From down below, two hundred paces away, came Chidiock's voice, clear and strong.

"I have sinned, and I beg your forgiveness. I beg forgiveness from my dear Queen, against whom I have committed such foul crimes, though I swear that I never intended her person harm. I beg forgiveness from all of my dear family, I beg forgiveness from my Lord Hatton, who placed his trust in me and which I so foully abused. I apologise to my company of Yeomen, that one of their number have engaged in such wicked treachery. And now I pray to God for forgiveness and I commit my soul to Him."

Anne stared as a dark-clad figure approached. She had not been able to watch the start of Babington's execution, and so was unsure what was now happening.

"Who is that?",

"'Tis the vicar, he will give a final blessing."

And then came the executioner, in short black hose, now wearing a black mask that covered all his head save the eyes. And Anne looked away, and glanced back for a moment to see Chidiock being raised to the gallows. How could the executioner honour his promise, in front of this raging crowd? There must be some trick, they must support his body somehow, so the noose did not tighten on his neck even though he appeared to fall and be hanged.

"I know he will be saved, but I cannot bear to watch," Anne cried, and she looked away at the ground as the mob roared. Only when the bloodlust of their howls had faded to silence did she dare to lift

her
head
and look
again, and
now she
saw Chidiock
lying on a
wooden block, the
executioner poised
with a long, curved
knife above him. She
gripped Jane's hand,
steeling herself to watch,

for this trick was the one of which she had been told. The knife descended and an inhuman scream rent the air, louder and louder, and then the crowd broke its silence and started to roar for more blood. And now Anne was sure: the scream was so different from the one she had heard a few minutes before when poor Babington had been cut – surely everyone else could tell that the cry was a chicken's, and that the knife was cutting harmlessly in the space between Chidiock's chest and his arm, releasing the bladder of pig's blood that flowed across the block and into the ground. She lifted her arms into the air, still holding Jane's hand, and cried out in elation: "We've done it!" and then lowering her voice to a whisper, added, "Chidiock is saved!"

"I pray so," said Jane, "but it all looked so horribly, horribly real."

Anne gazed around at the crowd, amazed and thankful that they had been fooled by the executioner's tricks, and even as she looked at the faces contorted with the strange lust of enjoyment at another person's pain, she saw a disturbance. Lower down the hill, near to the scaffold, a group of heavily armed men on horseback was moving among the onlookers, pushing people aside heedless of their angry cries. For a moment, she stared as though it was just one more part of the spectacle that did not concern her.

The leading rider's livery seemed to be all black, but as Anne watched she saw a glint where the sun caught something silver on it. "They're coming for me!" She gripped Jane's hand so tight that her sister winced, and as she released it she swung herself without pausing onto Bayard's back. "That's William Arundell's livery! He must be there, with his men-at arms! We must go!"

Jane mounted her horse as well, saying, "They are searching back and forth through the crowd, 'twill take them some minutes, there must be a thousand people between us and them. Put up thy hood, and let's slip away. The Fleet river will take us all the way down to the Thames at Blackfriars, so we should reach our rendezvous unseen."

They moved quietly back to the secret staircase, and as they reached the stream, Jane said, "I am so happy that thy madness has passed, and that you have abandoned any idea of meeting William!"

Anne shook her head. "I have not changed my mind. I am still determined to find him, but while we were on the hill, I realised there is a much better place."

She saw Jane staring at her with mouth open as she said, "There can be no place that is good to meet him! Ye must come with me and Chidiock to France. That is the only way. If you stay in England, they will track you down and arrest you, sooner or later."
"Come with you?" Anne began to shiver all over, even in the warmth of her woollen riding-kirtle, as she understood what this meant. "But I would never see the rest of the family again! I would never go back to Athelhampton!"

"Nor would you ever, if they take you to the Tower," muttered Jane. "Let us give Heynes the deed, he can find some innocent person to take it to William, and you can escape to France."

But Anne shook her head. They were now on the

stretch of water below the Bishop's Palace, and the stench of foul ordure worsened with every step. "If 'twas a proper court of law, anyone could take it," she said. "But that is not what they intend for Henry. There will be no chance for evidence, he will simply be condemned."

"But then, what point is there in running this mad risk to give the document to William?"

"He will not accept it from anyone, save myself. That is what he told me," Anne said. "He does this as some kind of favour to me, it is not an ordinary kind of legal process."

The stink was now so intense that Anne tightened the drawstring on her hood so it covered her mouth. They rode on slowly, Anne trying not to splash the muck up onto the upper part of Bayard's legs or her kirtle, but try as she might, her boots became covered in the filth. Now she saw that the stream was widening, and ahead a vista of sky and clear water appeared. "There is the Thames," she said, "soon we will be with Chidiock!"

They rode up a slope out of the stream. Ahead of them, a great archway was set in a high wall, with a servant in blue and gold livery standing on either side, and the same colours on an awning above.

"Is this Blackfriars?" asked Anne, frowning. "With those bright colours, it seems more like a fine house than a monastery. Have we come to the wrong place?"

"Chidiock and I passed by here, when we rode out together to enjoy the air, one fine morning. He told me that the monks are long gone, and 'tis now the dwelling of a great Lord," said Jane. "And here we must wait, but let us stand in the shadows, and keep our heads low, lest William's men-at-arms ride by."

They waited, and Anne became thirsty, and the sun moved down in the sky. She looked back at the way they had taken along the Fleet river, lest William's men came down it in pursuit of her, but Jane said, "No-one in London knows that route. And they don't know we are meeting here, so we should be safe for a while."

Merchants rode by on their fine horses, and carts filled with barrels and sacks, and yeomen in fine doublets and ruffians in rags, and more and more seemed to sway with drink. "The executions must be finished," said Anne, "these men look to me to have been watching and drinking, and are bound for home." A group of men-at-arms went by, but they did not sport the Arundell livery and paid no attention to them.

A tall man on a brown horse appeared in the distance, and as he approached, Anne realised it was the Captain. "Where is Chidiock?" she cried, but as he approached she saw his sober face and guessed the answer. She felt herself starting to shake all over, and she stretched out her hand to Jane, who had started sobbing, and drew her close.

Heynes spoke, quietly. "He is dead. I went to see the body, to avoid any suspicion, for it is the tradition that someone representing the family looks before the brutes take his head. I thought it would be some unknown corpse, put there in Chidiock's stead. But it was him."

Anne felt the cobbles collapsing under her feet and found herself leaning against the warm familiarity of Bayard's flanks with its comforting smell of sweat, and she said, "We have been betrayed!"

"Aye, that foul executioner played us false. He spared Chidiock the agonies, I saw from the corpse that death was swift and painless, but he took a life that he'd promised to save, and that cannot go unavenged. We will seek him out and finish him off."

Anne remembered the widening of Jane's eyes and the glow on her skin when she had first spoken of Chidiock, back even before their betrothal party. She remembered how they had looked at one another when they took their wedding vows, and she remembered them dancing together at the Harvest Supper in the Great Hall.

And she remembered how she had promised to Jane that she would save him, and now she had failed.

"You must go." Jane spoke quietly. "Nothing can bring back the dead. You must look to thyself now, and take ship for France. The cousins who were to have met me will look after thee."

"'Tis good counsel," said the Captain. "When I viewed poor Chidiock's body, there stood nearby two men with Arundell colours, and they marked the road I took. I fear they will have gathered their fellows and will follow us. They will come soon. If ye stay here, they will take ye."

Jane was still silent, but she looked at Anne and nodded.

"The dock is two hundred paces," said the Captain, his finger pointing down to a wooden jetty alongside which a wherry bobbed in the water. "Ye can be safe away within minutes – and with Bayard, too."

Anne had no strength in her limbs. Bayard, beside her, turned his head in the direction the Captain indicated and brayed gently. She had but to say the word and he would take her to the dockside, where she could board the boat and be safe.

She looked the opposite way along the river from the dock, and saw the great twin towers that she had seen from the hillside. She felt something in her fingers, and she looked down. There was nothing to see, but she could feel a small, furry hand in her own, as clear as in the days when Endy had been beside her. She stood up straight, strength regained, and spoke loud and clear.

"I will not run. I have done nothing that I know to be wrong. And though poor Chidiock is gone, there is still a chance to save Henry." She put out her hands and heaved herself onto Bayard, taking the reins.

"Anne!" cried Jane, her voice weak but clear. "You must go to France! I do not wish to lose you as well as Chidiock!"

"You will never see me again, if I take ship," said Anne, and she had a sensation of a weight on her back, and she remembered the harness of fine hemp that she had worn to carry Endy when she went riding. "I will stay. You remember what Friar Wytterage taught us, about the rules of Canon law? They are not allowed to arrest you on Church land."

"But ye cannot stay in a churchyard forever!"

Heynes cried. "'Tis a sanctuary used by petty criminals, sometimes if they have luck they may tarry there till nightfall and then slide away in the dark, when the Justices lose interest in them. But 'twill not work for ye, William will watch the gate day and night, till ye is driven out by hunger!"

"I am not going to sanctuary to escape," said Anne, "I am going there to fight."

Bayard was still turned towards the dock, as though determined to take her to the river. She leant down and spoke in his ear. "To Sanctuary – at Westminster Abbey."

The great horse turned his head away from the river, and onto the broad road that led towards Westminster.

Chapter 22
Westminster Abbey

Westminster Abbey filled the sky ahead of her, and an image came into Anne's mind of the picture of it in an old monkish book that Friar Wytterage had once showed her. She had not looked back since leaving Blackfriars, but she guessed that William and his men might not be too far behind, and at least once she heard a cry that reminded her of the brutish Walter, egging the others on. But the sensation of Endy on her back was stronger than ever, and she knew that Bayard would outpace the men-at-arms with ease.

A broad swathe of grass separated her from the famous church, and Bayard broke into a canter across this. Ahead was a gateway in a high wall, its great wooden door open but a low wicket blocking the way through. Bayard barely paused as he leapt across this, Anne ducking to keep her head below the arch, and once through they came to a halt in a large cobbled courtyard, bounded on three sides by ancient buildings and high walls, and on the fourth by the towers of the Abbey that rose into the mist of the smoky London air.

Monks and clergymen strode about quietly but purposefully, and for a moment Anne found herself wondering how they could be there after old Sir John

and his fellows had closed down all the monasteries for King Henry, before her attention was drawn to a commotion at the gateway.

Walter and his fellow thugs had arrived on the other side of the picket, where they waited, swords and pikes ready, blocking the way out and sneering at her; in their midst, she saw William dismounting, lifting off his sword and handing it to one of his men before opening the wicket gate, coming through the archway and walking across the courtyard towards her.

"Mistress Anne, you may have won a battle, but you won't win the war," he said. "We can't arrest you on this sacred soil, but my men will maintain guard and you will be trapped here, until you leave of your own accord."

"I am not here to stay," she said quietly. "I am here to right the wrongs you try to do." She had dismounted now, and she stood facing William, her hands on her hips.

"You may be young," said William, "but your crimes against Her Majesty are deserving of the punishment that comes to all who betray her – however hard they strive to escape."

"You may arrest me later, if that is the way it is to be, but first, I have the parchment I promised you. It proves the innocence of Henry."

William gave a low laugh, which seemed to Anne sad rather than mocking. "You claimed that before, but could produce nothing. I would not needlessly deprive you of another brother, but the law must be enforced."

Anne breathed deep, and prayed that she could

keep her eyes on William without blinking. "Here is the parchment," she said. She reached into Bayard's saddlebag, drew out the deed and held it out to William, who took it and started to read out loud.

"*A Deed, for the purchase of the Old Manor at Almer, in Dorsetshire, sold by Christopher Anketill, Guardian of Brownsea Island for Sir Christopher Hutton, to Chidiock Tichborne, the payment by Henry Brune of Lydlinch, Dorsetshire... Dated 15th February, 1586... signed and witnessed, Henry Brune, Christopher Anketill and Chidiock Tichborne.*"* William looked at her, saying, "Where did you find this?"

"I found it, in a strange place.... in a secret cupboard at Athelhampton, where Jane and Chidiock had been staying. And... that gold never reached the plotters, it is at Athelhampton."

William said, "'Tis a pity that you turned down my offer of service to the Queen, for I think you would be good at finding out secrets."

He rolled up the parchment, putting it inside his doublet, and Anne felt a pain in her heart at the thought that he might simply walk off and throw it away. But instead he took a step closer towards her and continued in a low tone, "There is law, and then there is politics. The exposure of the plotters was important. But much, much more important, is that Mary wrote a letter to Babington, the man who led poor Chidiock into that terrible web."

He moved even nearer, his voice quieter than when Frances had whispered household secrets to her in the days when she was tiny, and she realised that he did not want Walter or anyone else to hear what he was saying. "That letter written by Mary implicates her in Babington's plot – it is her death warrant." He was so close to her that Anne could see the individual hairs on his head. "There is no need of more. Babington and Chidiock and the other four have served their purpose."

He paused, and Anne found herself gasping to take in great gulps of air as though she had been underwater and was just surfacing, for he continued, louder now: "Our good Queen is not vindictive, 'tis one of her many great strengths. It makes no difference now, whether Henry was part of this plot, or not. This parchment may speak true, it may speak false, it matters not. It is a good enough reason to set him free."

Anne realised that Walter had crept up close enough to hear William's most recent words, for he let out a low, guttural noise, and muttered, "Her dastardly brother Henry may escape, but she cannot. We have chased her half across London and now we have her! She bribed the executioner to save the traitor Chidiock – we have the evidence. She must go to the Tower!"

Walter gave a sign and one of his men approached, holding a small bag besmirched with blood and dragging a man with bruises across his face. Anne felt nauseous as she recognised the executioner – and the pouch that held her pearls. Walter took it and opened the drawstring, saying, "Here is the evidence! These are her pearls, no-one else in the land has any as fine – they were bequeathed to her by her grandmother, who got them as a gift from our good Queen. My Lord, you told me to find proof of her guilt, and this is beyond doubt!"

Anne thought of Ma Melemouth's warnings. Young John had restored those pearls to her not as an act of death-bed redemption, but to hurt her, in a far more deadly way than by playing with her hopes of attracting a husband. She shouted at Walter, "The executioner was ready to take just gold – but you told him to demand the pearls! That was Young John's plan – and you did what he told you to do!"

Walter leered at her. "All I did was tell him that the pearls had been restored to their rightful owner! When he heard that, 'twas he who decided to demand them from you, and you who gave them to him. 'Tis you and he who are guilty." Anne saw William gazing sadly at her, and she felt sure he was about to turn and walk away, leaving her with no route out of the courtyard save to the Tower. She started to lose her balance and had to lean against the side of Bayard to avoid collapsing onto the cobbles of the courtyard.

From somewhere, she heard the roar that Endy had made when he had defended her at Athelhampton against Walter and his villainous friend, even though they towered over him. She looked at the horrible expression on Walter's face and it suddenly felt like the spark from a tinder-box, igniting her despair over Chidiock into a surge of energy that ran up her whole body and exploded into a memory of what Jane had told her about the Queen's edict.

She took her hands off the side of Bayard, stood up straight and found with surprise that her height matched Walter's. She had grown since she first met him, when she had looked down at him only in her mind's eye. Now her defiant stare went directly into his mean grey eyes, which turned away as she looked at him.

"I was carrying out the Queen's command!" she cried, praying quietly that what Jane had been told by the man from Hampton Court had been true.

Walter stared at her in silence, and Anne guessed that he could not even understand what she meant, but as she looked at William she saw the edges of his mouth begin to move up, and slowly a smile spread across his face.

"The Queen issued an edict," Anne continued. "The plotters were to be hanged till dead, and only their dead flesh was to be tormented. I knew this command had not reached the executioner, and I gave him the pearls to make sure he honoured it!" This, she thought, was not a strictly accurate description of the agreement she had made, but she now understood that William was looking for some way to let her go.

The executioner looked up and caught Anne's gaze for a moment, and then he stared back at the ground as he spoke. "That's what we agreed," he said. "I saved 'im from the suffering, using a trick that I 'ave." Anne realised that he had understood he must tell the same story as her to save himself, even if the bit about their bargain wasn't exactly true. He continued: "When the knife went into 'im 'e was dead already, 'twas the chicken's cry that everyone heard. I made sure 'e was dead on the gallows, so 'e didn't suffer."

William turned to look at her, and she saw that the lines round his jaw had disappeared as he nodded and spoke softly and slowly. "In Dorchester, with the pitch, you took to heart those words we had together under the tree at Athelhampton."

"I would never spy for you on my family," said Anne, "but I would always strive to stop evil against Her Majesty."

"As for the execution," William said, the hint of a smile on his face, "our good Queen asked that the edict be delayed and not used till tomorrow. That was her intent. But ... in a legal sense, technically, it was valid today. So, you have simply ensured that the law was applied." He nodded again, and made some signal to his entourage, who put down their weapons and stood back from the boundary of the sanctuary so the way out was no longer blocked. Walter stood between her and the gate and was the last to move out of the way and Anne saw his scowl deepening, but she knew that it was a sign that he – and Young John – had been defeated.

Anne sensed in William's eye something familiar from that exchange in the shade by the lawn, the strange sense of closeness when he'd told her he would never marry, and as the threat of the Tower faded, she was suddenly emboldened to ask for more.

"And I want my pearls back!" She looked at the executioner, whose eyes stared away from her, down at the great flagstones of the sanctuary court. "He has all the gold, he only demanded the pearls when Walter suggested it. Really he is owed nothing, since he was just obeying the Queen's command!"

William was silent but Anne felt his eyes looking straight at her and she stared boldly back, and then she saw him turn to Walter, lift his hand and point at the bloody bag. Walter, with a low growl like an animal in pain, extended his arm and gave it to Anne.

Anne thrust it into her saddlebag, her breath racing as she thought how close Young John, even in death, had come to using the pearls to destroy her. Now, she had the gift that had been promised to her, and she could use it as she wished, for her dowry, or to keep and wear as her Grandma had done, or simply to give away.

She swung herself onto Bayard's back, looking briefly at Walter, at William, and the armed men, who all seemed to be standing frozen, as though in shock at how everything had changed. She urged Bayard through the arch out of the sanctuary, which now lay clear and open, and they were away.

Epilogue

In the deep shadows of the parlour at midnight, Gyb's green eyes glinted in the glow from the embers in the fireplace. Anne, still in her muddy riding-kirtle, sat at the table with Lizzie, a single candle between them.

"Jane sobs quietly, when she thinks she's alone," whispered Lizzie. "She stops when she realises someone's there, but I've heard her several times."

"'Tis for the best," said Anne quietly, "she loved Chidiock so much, 'tis right that she lets her sadness out."

"And next year, when her mourning is over, her tears will eventually begin to ebb, and then she need not be alone. In the kitchen, there is talk that a gentleman from the Isle of Wight has already written to thy father about her."

"And what of Eliza and Henry?"

"They're so happy! Henry arrived from London three days ago, I was amazed that he got out of the Tower so swiftly. He came back home before thee!"

"I had to rest. The good Baron Dacre and his daughter looked after me, I just sat quietly and watched the river and thought of Chidiock – and before I knew it, five days had passed. But I'm so glad they let Henry out quickly."

"Thy suitor William," said Lizzie, with a

mischievous smile, "must be very powerful. Henry said that he came to the Tower himself, with some special warrant, and the jailers opened the door of his cell at once!"

"He's not my suitor!" Anne said as loudly as she could while still whispering, and flicked some congealed candle wax at Lizzie. "And nor does he want to be. But he seems to rather like me, as I him, but not for marriage."

Lizzie dodged the wax, laughing quietly, and said, "And what of the pearls? Did the executioner keep them? Or did William confiscate them?"

"No – I made them give them back to me." She took them out of her purse and laid them on the table, where they seemed to sparkle in the candlelight. "But, though they came from Grandma, I'm not sure I really want them any more. They're spoiled, somehow, by the evil that Young John tried to do with them."

"Well…" Lizzie hesitated, before continuing, "I have something for thee, 'tis as nothing compared to thy pearls, but it has no bad things in its past. 'Tis what I promised, before you set off for London." She put her hand to her waist and brought up a small pouch, made of hessian cut from a sack, which she put into Anne's hand, squeezing it between both of her own. "I kept it for you, while you were away," she whispered, "I was hoping and praying that you would come home safe, and I waited to be ready to give it to you."

Anne opened the pouch, and took out the bracelet. It was made of cheap tin, but well worked, with markings by a craftsman. She put it on her wrist, stood up, and embraced Lizzie, so close that she could scarcely breathe. "'Tis as I said when you first told me of it. 'Twill be the most precious thing I have. More precious than the pearls."

Anne saw Lizzie looking away, and realised that her friend did not believe her - and on impulse, she said, "And to prove it, I'm going to give the pearls away."

She put the bracelet on her wrist and shoved the pearls, roughly, to the far side of the table.

Lizzie looked at her, full in the eyes. "Give them away? How can you do that? The Queen's pearls! Who would you give them to?"

Anne took her friend's hands. "My Grandmother Joan is giving her money to my Uncle Nicholas, so he can set up a new college at the university in Oxford. I'm going to write to them and say I'm giving the pearls to help." Anne paused, running her hand across the bracelet, and then across the pearls. "And ... Father's leaving Athelhampton to me and my four sisters, not some distant male relative, so I'm going to follow his lead. I'll ask that the money from the pearls be used to let women be teachers, and be educated, alongside the men. And to help people go there who don't have enough money to pay."

"Don't be silly! Women teachers? How could that be? The good Friar told us, all the teachers at Oxford have to enter Holy Orders. So, they have to be men!"

"I don't see why that rule can't be changed. Things won't get better unless people push for them to be improved!"

Anne was quiet for a moment, before adding,

"Young John let me have those pearls to trap me and have me sent to the Tower – and other people tried to attack me and steal them. I've escaped all of that, and used them to help spare Chidiock from the horrid things they would have done to him. Now, I'm going to make sure they do something good for the future, that will last for ages and ages and help lots of people!"

Historical Notes

While this book is a work of fiction, all the main characters are based on real historical figures. Many of the key events are based on well-documented history, and you can still visit most of the places mentioned in both Dorset and London.

Anne herself, her parents, sisters, aunts and uncles are all real historical characters. You can visit Athelhampton House today and walk through the rooms that they lived in, including the Great Hall, the Marriage Chamber, and the Elizabethan kitchen with its great brick arch. You can still watch doves flying in and out of the dovecote, just as Anne does in the book.

There really was a raid planned by the Duc de Guise on the Dorset coast, with evidence that John Williams of Tyneham, Henry Brune's brother-in-law, was involved. It never did take place – though history does not tell us that it was Anne Martyn who stopped it. Tyneham was demolished by the Army in the 1960s but you can visit the nearby "ghost" village, and its main entrance arch is preserved in the gardens at Athelhampton. You can walk across the old stone bridge at Wool that Anne had to cross to get to Tyneham, and see the nearby buildings mentioned in the book; further upstream along the Frome river you can see the "Symonds Castle" and even rent it for a holiday.

"Old" Sir John Tregonwell served Queen Elizabeth, as well as her three predecessors, and helped arrange the divorce that allowed her parents to marry. So it's not implausible that his wife, the Lady Elizabeth, would have been given a generous gift like pearls by the Queen. The house where Sir John and the Lady Elizabeth lived was replaced centuries ago, but you can still visit the adjacent Milton Abbey.

The Lady Elizabeth really did sadly pass away shortly before the events in this book, and her house was inherited by her grandson "Young" Sir John Tregonwell, with whom she and the Martyns had a well-documented long-running feud. He died shortly after his grandmother, as described in the book. Evidence from Star Chamber proceedings relates how his servant Walter Bearde was one of the leaders in an armed struggle over a barn that Young John instigated.

The Martyn family really did spend the Twelve Days of Yuletide with the Arundells at Wardour Castle in 1584 (documented by the report in the Crown Papers interrogation of Chidiock's servant), where there is a room in the dining hall believed to be a hidden chapel for Mass. So, Anne Martyn and William Arundell almost certainly would have met, though history does not record how their relationship developed.

The Arundells were a family divided among themselves, with William spying on his uncle who lived in France and plotted against Queen Elizabeth; though whether William was as powerful as in the book is not documented.

Captain Stephen Heynes was a famous Dorsetshire pirate who really was reported drowned in the Bay of Biscay shortly before many other pirates were hanged. His Bosun and wife ran an inn at Corfe Castle, as described in the book, though the current pubs in the village were built after the Tudor era.

John Blanke, a trumpet-player from Africa, is believed to have been part of Catherine of Aragon's entourage when she landed at Plymouth in 1501. She was met by a delegation of Knights, thought to have included Sir William Martyn, who would probably have invited her to stay at Athelhampton as one of the stopovers during her month's journey of 180 miles to meet her future husband. Blanke married in 1512, though the son described in the book is not recorded.

Chidiock Tichborne was one of the Babington plotters, and there is extensive evidence that he was married to Jane Martyn, including the reports in the Crown Papers of the interrogation of his servant. The poem that he wrote to his wife the night before his execution is well-known. It was addressed to Agnes, which as explained in the book, in Tudor times was pronounced in almost the same way as Jane, and was a nickname used for devout women.

Chidiock and Jane did live at Almer Manor, which nowadays is a private house and can only be viewed from the nearby churchyard. They rented it from the steward of Sir Christopher Hatton, who was Chidiock's commanding officer in the Yeomanry – and who did nothing to save him. Queen Elizabeth gave him the former Bishop of Ely's palace in London, right by the Fleet river, which Anne and Jane ride along in the book. The palace is remembered today in the name of the famous road Hatton Garden at the heart of the jewellery district, while the river is now underground.

Henry Brune really was arrested alongside the Babington plotters and held in the Tower, but was subsequently released – though history does not record whether Anne Martyn caused this to happen.

Queen Elizabeth really did command that those involved in the Babington plot executed on the second day should be hanged until dead before being butchered; history does not relate whether she had already issued this edict the day before.

Anne's uncle Nicholas Wadham really did plan for a new Oxford college, using funds he would inherit from her grandmother Joan. Exceptionally for the Tudor era, he stipulated that the teachers (fellows) did not need to take Holy Orders, just as Anne wants him to in the book (though there's no record of him asking for women to be admitted). After Nicholas' death, his widow completed the project, though she was unable to reach agreement on secular teachers. Centuries later, this was allowed and after even more delay, women were admitted as teachers and students.

Acknowledgements

The inspiration for this book comes from the highways and byways of Dorset and beyond, where so many traces of the Elizabethan years can still be found by those who search; and especially from Athelhampton House, with its magical, half-millennial old rooms and secret passages and its friendly ghosts who never seem too far away when the light starts to fade; and from the many generations of the Martyn family who built Athelhampton and lived there throughout the Tudor era, and whose descendants remained connected with the house for hundreds of years.

Great thanks are due to Noah Warnes, for the amazing illustrations that really bring Anne, William and everyone else alive; to Jonathan Eyers, whose editorial guidance helped me develop my early drafts; to David Williams, who gave outstanding inspiration on marketing; to Owen Davies, who not only provided great advice on the complex history of the Martyn family, their marriage alliances, and Athelhampton House itself, but also laid out the entire book and arranged printing by the local Dorset firm of Henry Ling; and to the many others at Athelhampton who gave invaluable input.

And I owe enormous thanks to Henrietta Irving, my wonderful and beautiful partner, whose warm encouragement persuaded me that the early drafts of the first Anne of Athelhampton book were worth developing and whose support has been invaluable throughout the whole project.

About the Illustrator

Noah Warnes

Noah grew up in the wilds of Dorset, surrounded by art materials and never far from his drum kit. He's passionately creative, drawing every day and researching new methods to make art. Noah currently lives in Falmouth, Cornwall.

You can see more of his work at
www.noahwarnes.com.

About the Author

Giles Keating

Giles fell in love with Athelhampton when he first arrived at its ancient riverside setting amidst Dorset's rolling hills, and he became part of the team that welcomes visitors to its Tudor house and classic gardens.

Giles worked for several decades as an economist at the University of London and in the City, crunching numbers and meeting people from all over the world, to try and get some insight into where the great events of the time might lead – the collapse of the Berlin Wall, the rise of the internet, the growth in the power of China, the looming climate disaster.

"All of these are very important, but some readers might find them a bit dry. The Anne of Athelhampton books are about things that arguably matter even more – and certainly more fun to read about."

Athelhampton House
as it today

Athelhampton House nestles in the heart of Dorset, a few miles east of the county town of Dorchester. It is considered one of the finest examples of Tudor domestic architecture in England.

When you visit the house today, you will find the Great Hall, the Minstrels' Gallery, the Marriage Chamber and many other rooms much as Anne would have seen them. In the newly-restored Elizabethan kitchen, you can see big pots for cooking pottage of the kind that Anne helped Lizzie to stir, and in the Screens Passage you can peer through the murk of the Screens Passage and maybe see a ghostly figure as she did.

Outdoors, the house is surrounded by award-winning gardens built in the Elizabethan manner by the enigmatic Victorian Alfred Cart de Lafontaine. You can sit by the dovecote, where Anne sat with William, and wander through the kitchen garden as she did with Eliza. This has been rebuilt over the centuries but still provides fruit and vegetables for people in the house. You can even eat some of that food yourself in the cafe, housed in a building on the site of the stables where Anne learnt she was to be given Bayard.

The house and its gardens welcome visitors across all seasons of the year.

For current opening times,
please visit www.athelhampton.co.uk
or telephone 01305 848363.

Anne of Athelhampton
and the
Riddle of the Apes

Volume 1 in the Anne of Athelhampton Trilogy

Why has Anne been given a pet ape, as a twelfth birthday gift from her grasping cousin Young John? Can he solve the riddle before Anne, and use it to accuse their grandmother, the Lady Elizabeth, of witchcraft and of harbouring a priest?

Helped by Endy and her friends Lizzie and Robert, Anne searches the passageways and walls of her family home, to reveal their secrets and solve the riddle.

Only to to discover that she herself is Young John's target, and that her struggle against him will lead her into mortal danger…

Available to order in all bookshops, in person at Athelhampton House or online at www.athelhampton.co.uk

Anne of Athelhampton
and the
Tincture of the Roses

Volume 3 in the Anne of Athelhampton Trilogy

In preparation - watch for announcements at
www.athelhampton.com/anne and on social media

Books available from the Athelhampton Press

Anne of Athelhampton
and the
Riddle of the Apes

Giles Keating

Illustrated by
Noah Warnes

ISBN 978-0-9555815-1-9

Athelhampton, The Gardens

Sophy Davies, Owen Davies & Giles Keating

ISBN 979-0-0-9555815-8-8

Athelhampton, The House

Owen Davies & Giles Keating

ISBN 978-0-9555815-6-4

The Visitation to Athelhampton Hall

Alfred Cart de Lafontaine & Owen Davies

ISBN 978-0-9555815-3-3

Gyb the Cat Anne of Athelhampton Colouring Book

Noah Warnes

ISBN 978-0-9555815-7-1

Available to order in all bookshops, in person at
Athelhampton House or online at www.athelhampton.co.uk

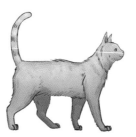